THE THIRD MUSHROOM

More Novels by Jennifer L. Holm

The Fourteenth Goldfish

Full of Beans

Turtle in Paradise

Middle School Is Worse Than Meatloaf

Eighth Grade Is Making Me Sick

Penny from Heaven

The Boston Jane series

The May Amelia books

By Jennifer L. Holm and Matthew Holm

Babymouse: Tales from the Locker

The Babymouse series

The Squish series

The Sunny series

My First Comics series

The Comics Squad series (with Jarrett J. Krosoczka)

THE
THIRD
MUSHROOM

JENNIFER L. HOLM

A Yearling Book

Text copyright © 2018 by Jennifer L. Holm
Cover art copyright © 2020 by Tad Carpenter
Interior illustrations copyright © 2018 by Tad Carpenter

All rights reserved. Published in the United States by Yearling, an imprint of Random House Children's Books, a division of Penguin Random House LLC, New York. Originally published in hardcover in the United States by Random House Children's Books, a division of Penguin Random House LLC, New York, in 2018.

Yearling and the jumping horse design are registered trademarks of Penguin Random House LLC.

Photograph credits: p. 215 © Jennifer L. Holm, p. 218 © Science History Images/Alamy Stock Photo, p. 221 © Keystone Pictures USA/Alamy Stock Photo, p. 223 © Pictorial Press Ltd/Alamy Stock Photo, p. 225 © Classic Image/Alamy Stock Photo, p. 227 © Pictorial Press Ltd/Alamy Stock Photo, p. 229 © Alan King engraving/Alamy Stock Photo.

Visit us on the Web! rhcbooks.com

Educators and librarians, for a variety of teaching tools, visit us at RHTeachersLibrarians.com

The Library of Congress has cataloged the hardcover edition of this work as follows:
Name: Holm, Jennifer L., author.
Title: The third mushroom / Jennifer L. Holm.
Description: First edition. | New York : Random House, [2018] | Summary: When thirteen-year-old Ellie's grandpa Melvin, a world-renowned scientist in the body of a fourteen-year-old boy, comes for an extended visit, he teaches her that experimenting—and failing—is part of life.
Identifiers: LCCN 2017043070 | ISBN 978-1-5247-1980-7 (hardcover) |
ISBN 978-1-5247-1981-4 (lib. bdg.) | ISBN 978-1-5247-1982-1 (ebook)
Subjects: | CYAC: Grandfathers—Fiction. | Scientists—Fiction. | Aging—Fiction. | Middle schools—Fiction. | Schools—Fiction. | Friendship—Fiction. | Family life—Fiction.
Classification: LCC PZ7.H732226 Thi 2018 | DDC [Fic]—dc23

ISBN 978-1-5247-1983-8 (paperback)

Printed in the United States of America
10 9 8 7 6 5 4 3 2 1
First Yearling Edition 2020

Random House Children's Books supports the First Amendment and celebrates the right to read.

For Mr. Frink

Contents

One sometimes finds what one is not looking for.

—Alexander Fleming

Mushroom War

Maybe it's because I'm an only child, but my parents have always been a little obsessed with my eating. They insist that I try everything on my plate. That I eat what they eat. No chicken tenders off the kids' menu for me. If they have calamari or chicken livers, that's what I have to eat, too.

And the truth is: I'm a pretty good eater. Growing up in the Bay Area, you get to try a lot of different kinds of cuisine. I've had Indian, Burmese, Mexican, Chinese, Peruvian, Vietnamese, you name it. I even like the raw-fish kind of sushi.

My parents agree that I've never been really picky except when it comes to one thing.

Mushrooms.

The first time I tried a mushroom I was in kindergarten. My parents are divorced, but they've always stayed good friends, and we have family dinner once a week.

We were at a favorite Italian restaurant and my mother had ordered a pasta dish for the table—ravioli. I loved pasta of all kinds, so I was happy.

Then I took a bite.

To my horror, instead of creamy cheese being in the cute pasta pocket, there were weird brown chunks. It tasted awful. Like dirt.

"What is this?" I asked my mom.

"Mushroom ravioli. Don't you like it?"

I shook my head. I definitely did *not* like it.

My parents seemed a little disappointed.

The second time I tried a mushroom, it was at a Chinese restaurant. We'd gone to see a play and it was late and I was really hungry. My parents talked me into ordering a chicken-and-mushroom dish.

Try new things, they told me.

But this time the mushroom had a horrible texture: rubbery and slimy. What was the deal with mushrooms, anyway? Why were they so gross?

I didn't starve (I ate the plain rice and fortune cookies), but I was annoyed. At the mushrooms. And at myself for trying them again.

Then and there I resolved never to eat another mushroom.

That's when the Mushroom War started.

Because my parents took it as a personal challenge that I didn't like mushrooms. They started putting them in everything. They put mushrooms in stir-fry and lasagna and salad. I guess they figured I'd cave and eat them.

But there was no way I was making *that* mistake again.

Eventually, my parents gave up and I won the Mushroom War. They moved on to brussels sprouts, which didn't deserve such a bad rap, in my opinion.

As the years went by, they would occasionally

serve me something with mushrooms. And every single time, I picked them out and left them in a neat pile on the side of my plate.

At least no one could say I didn't have good table manners.

Criminal

My mom and I like to watch courtroom dramas on TV. She says they're great character studies. She loves the scenes with lawyers arguing, especially when they shout "Objection!" My mom's a high school theater teacher, so she's a fan of anything dramatic.

While the lawyers are interesting, my heart's been with the criminals lately. Because I know just how they feel. Middle school is like jail: the food is terrible, you're forced to exercise, and it's the same boring routine every day. Mostly it's the buildings that make you feel like a prisoner. There's no color, no style, and everything smells like dirty socks.

The only exceptions are the science classrooms. They redid the labs over the summer, and now they look like the Hollywood version of a high-tech lab. But my science teacher, Mr. Ham, doesn't look anything like a Hollywood scientist. He's young and likes to wear loud, silly ties instead of a lab coat. This is the second year in a row I've had him, because he moved up a grade.

"We'll be hosting the county science fair this spring," he announces. "I'd encourage you all to enter. You'll earn extra credit. It's also fine if you want to buddy up with another student and enter as a team."

Even though I've already got a good grade in class, I'm tempted because of my grandfather. I know he'd want me to enter: he's a scientist.

I haven't seen my grandpa Melvin in over a year. He's been traveling across the country, visiting places by bus, on an extended vacation. I miss everything about him. His old-man fashion style of wearing black socks. How he always orders moo goo gai pan at Chinese restaurants and steals the packets of soy sauce. Most of all, I miss talking to him. He's bossy and opinionated and thinks he's smarter than everyone else because he has two PhDs.

And maybe he is.

When the last bell of the day rings, everyone rushes out of the classrooms like criminals being released.

I spot Raj waiting for me by my locker; he's hard to miss. He's tall and lean and towers over most other kids. But that's not the only reason he stands out. Raj has the whole goth thing going on: he's got piercings and is dressed entirely in black, right down to his weathered Doc Martens. Even his thick hair is black. Well, except for the long blue streak in the front. It's striking and makes him look like a wizard.

"Hey," I say.

"So, you decided not to go for it, huh?" he asks, studying my hair.

It was my idea in the first place. I wanted a change of some kind. To maybe stand out. Look a little different. My hair is pretty boring, so I thought I would dye it. My mom was all for it. She's always dyeing her hair crazy colors and makes it look easy.

Still, I was nervous. It seemed like a big step.

Raj suggested I just get a streak in my hair. He said he'd do it, too. A buddy thing.

We endlessly debated colors. He liked the idea of red. I liked pink. We were both against green (it only looks good on leprechauns). Finally, we settled on blue.

But when I went to the hair salon this past weekend to get mine done, I panicked. What if it was a mistake? What if I looked terrible with a blue streak? Like a blue skunk?

In the end, I got my hair cut same as always (one inch) and no streak.

"I couldn't do it," I admit.

"That's okay," he says.

"You're not mad?"

"Of course not."

I feel better immediately. Raj wouldn't lie.

Because he's my best friend. I know his locker combination and he knows mine.

We didn't start out being best friends. But over the last year, it just kind of happened. My mom says having a best friend is like learning to speak a foreign language. You stumble around for the right words, and then one day it clicks and you understand everything.

"I've got a chess meet next week," Raj says. "I was wondering if you wanted to come? It's here at the school."

"Sure!" I say. I've never been to a chess match before.

He smiles. "Great. Well, I gotta roll. Chess club. Catch ya later."

"Bye," I say.

I watch as he disappears into the crowd.

o o o

Sometimes I wonder if my life would be different if I had a sibling. My parents can be a bit over-protective. I've noticed that the parents of big fami-lies are more laid-back. My old friend Brianna is the youngest of four, and when she turned ten, her mom let her stay home by herself. Me? I had a baby-sitter up until last year.

This year my mom finally caved on the sitter thing.

"But you have to text me the minute you get home from school." She made me promise her.

I'm not nervous about going home to an empty house after school, because I know Jonas is waiting for me.

Jonas is our cat.

Even though I'd always wanted a dog, Jonas was the perfect cat. He came to us litter-box trained and didn't claw the furniture. We got him at a local animal shelter called Nine Lives. The day we went, the place was filled with adorable kittens. But I couldn't take my eyes off the calm, older gray cat in the corner. There was something about him. The lady at the shelter said he'd been there for a while. He'd probably been abandoned by a person who'd moved away. It's crazy but true: people sometimes leave their animals behind like old sofas. We took him home that day.

Jonas is sitting on the front porch when I walk up the driveway. He twines around my legs.

"How's my favorite babysitter?" I ask him. It's our little joke.

I text my mom that I'm home and unlock the front door.

The house is quiet. I kick off my shoes and drop my keys in the junk bowl by the door. It's full of ticket stubs to movies, half-melted lipsticks, and single earrings missing their mates. Some boy stuff has made its way into the bowl since my mom married Ben: cuff links and dry cleaner tickets and wintergreen breath mints.

I head toward the kitchen. The smell of warmed-up cheese burritos lingers in the air. This seems odd to me. I'm the burrito eater, not my mom. Also, she's got rehearsals today after school for the new play.

"Mom?" I call, but no one answers.

As I approach the kitchen counter, I see an empty burrito box by the microwave. Next to it is a carton of almond milk.

I would never in a million years have left a carton of milk on the counter. That's when it hits me.

Someone is in the house!

And that *someone* is drinking our milk and eating our frozen burritos.

For a brief moment it seems cute, like Goldilocks and the Three Bears. Then my eyes land on the back door, which leads out onto our small deck. The glass has been smashed in around the handle, and it's all over the floor. That's when I realize this is no cute blond girl who has come into our house to try out porridge and beds. It's someone who breaks glass doors.

A real-life criminal.

I pull out my cell phone and dial quickly.

"This is 911. What is the nature of your emergency?" a perky voice asks.

"Someone's in my house," I whisper urgently.

"Are you by yourself?" the voice asks calmly.

"Yes! I mean, *no!*" I struggle to explain. "The person who broke in may still be in here! He ate the burritos!"

"Are you near an exit?"

I debate this for a second. I don't want to go out the broken back door in case the person is still there.

"Uh, yeah! The front door!"

"Try to get outside, and stay on the line with me."

"Roger that!" I whisper. It's something a cop would say. I think maybe I'm watching too much TV.

I creep down the hallway. I've almost reached the front door when I hear something that startles me so much that I freeze in my tracks: the sound of a toilet flushing.

The criminal is using our bathroom?

Then I hear splashing water hit the bathroom sink. *At least the criminal has good hygiene,* I think a little hysterically. I should be out the door, but my feet have frozen in place.

The bathroom door bangs open and I gasp.

A boy with long brown hair tied back in a pony-tail walks out, an annoyed expression on his face. He's wearing khaki pants, a button-down shirt, and loafers . . . with *black socks.*

"I need the plunger," he says. "The toilet's clogged."

The emergency operator's voice jolts me. "Are you still on the line?"

I exhale slowly and hold the phone to my ear.

"It's okay," I tell her. "It's just my grandfather."

Goldilocks

I assure the emergency operator that the stranger is actually my grandfather.

"Are you positive?" she asks me.

"He was in the bathroom the whole time," I say. She laughs.

"My dad's the same way," she says. "Must be an old-man thing."

Then I hang up and rush across the hallway.

"Grandpa!" I cry, and hug him tight.

He tolerates it for a moment, and then a thunderous expression crosses his face. "Did you know the key to the front door doesn't work anymore? I tried to squeeze in the cat door, but I couldn't fit. So I had to break in."

"Mom's not gonna be too happy about that."

"It's not my fault," he insists. "Who changed the locks?"

"Ben did. He's really into safety."

He snorts. "He can't be that 'into' safety if I broke in so easily."

My grandfather looks and sounds just like a belligerent teenager, even though he's really seventy-seven. I know it sounds bizarre, but my grandfather has figured out a way to reverse aging and has turned himself young again.

"Where's your babysitter?" he demands.

"Mom says I'm old enough to stay home by myself now," I explain. "I'm in seventh grade."

"Humph," he says. He makes a face as if to say he totally disagrees with my mother. But then again, my grandfather has never really agreed with her about anything. He's a die-hard scientist, and she went into theater. Talk about oil and water.

"I can't believe you're here!"

"Yes, well, I had laundry to do," he says.

"Laundry?"

"I've been living out of a suitcase for the last year. I have a *lot* of dirty laundry."

I look past him at the laundry room. He's not kidding. There's a towering pile of dirty clothes sitting on top of the washing machine.

"Also, I missed you," he says gruffly.

There's a loud knocking on the front door. When I open it, a police officer is standing there. She's tall and looks serious.

"You called 911?" she asks.

"Uh, yeah. Everything's fine, though."

My grandfather comes to the door. "Who is it?"

"It's the police," I whisper. "I called 911 before I realized it was you in the house."

"Who are you?" the policewoman asks, taking in my grandfather's long hair.

"I'm her cousin," he says.

This was the cover story he used when he lived here last year after he first turned himself young.

I think quickly. "My grandfather dropped him off, and he forgot his key."

"I see," she says. "Well, remember your key next time, okay?"

I answer for him. "He will!"

I watch as the patrol car drives away, my heart beating a million miles a minute. But my grandpa seems completely unfazed.

"Do you think there are any more of those frozen burritos left?" he asks me.

My grandfather stands at the kitchen counter eating another burrito.

"By the way, have any packages arrived for me?" he asks.

"One came a while ago. It was from the Philippines."

It arrived in a cooler with strict instructions to freeze it.

His face turns ashen. "What did you do with it?"

"I put it in the garage. In the deep freeze," I tell him.

"Good girl," he says. "By the way, have you seen my blog?"

"You have a blog? What's it called?"

"Www.MelvinSagarskyHasTwoPhDs.com."

That's a pretty good name for a blog.

Just then I hear the clunky rolling sound of the garage door opening. A minute later my mom walks in holding a bag from our favorite Chinese takeout place. Her hair is bleached white, and she's wearing one of her standard outfits: a fun plaid skirt paired with tall black boots and a T-shirt that says:

HAMLET: I SEE DEAD PEOPLE.

"Ellie! Did you leave that huge pile of stinky laundry on top of the washing machine? You know better than . . ." Her voice trails off.

"It's mine," my grandfather says.

My mother's mouth drops open. "Dad! You're home!"

"Excellent powers of observation," he says.

She shakes her head in bemusement. "You know, there's this crazy invention. It's called a cell phone. I seem to remember giving you one."

"You people spend your lives with your heads buried in those things. I can't be bothered. Also, the screen broke."

Still, my mom seems vaguely pleased to see him and gives him a hug.

"I think you got taller, Dad," she observes, ruffling his hair.

"Well, your skirts have gotten shorter! I can see your knees!"

My mom grimaces. "Then again, maybe you haven't grown up after all."

We settle around the kitchen table. My grandfather fishes through the takeout boxes. A cozy feeling settles in my stomach at seeing him sitting there.

"No moo goo gai pan?" he grumbles.

"We weren't exactly expecting you, Dad," my mom says.

He dumps a pile of lo mein onto his plate and starts picking around the noodles. "Where's the meat?"

"Ben's a vegetarian, so now we're all trying it," my mom says.

We're eating a lot of tofu these days. I'm not a huge fan; it's bland.

"Why don't you just try eating insects instead? Taste about as good," my grandfather mutters. "Where is this new husband of yours?"

"Ben's in India," she says. "It's just a short-term thing."

Ben's a video game designer, and he's supervising a studio of programmers in India working on their next major game. It's a big opportunity for him, but I know my mom misses him. I miss him, too. When Ben's around, we sit down as a family for dinner and actually talk. Since he's been gone, my mom and I have fallen back into our girls-only routine of eating too much takeout in front of the television.

Jonas sidles up to the table and leaps onto the empty chair, like he has a perfect right to be there. Then he meows loudly.

I put a piece of tofu on the table in front of him.

"Where did that beast come from?" my grand-father asks.

"His name is Jonas. After Jonas Salk," I say, knowing it will impress him. Jonas Salk is my favor-ite scientist. He developed the polio vaccine.

"I'm not a big believer in pets," my grandpa says. "Especially at the dinner table."

"You don't have to tell me. I spent my entire childhood begging for a dog," my mom says, losing some of her good humor. "So, how long are you planning on gracing us with your presence?"

"A few months," he says. "Maybe longer. It's hard to say."

I pass around the fortune cookies. My grandfather opens his and tosses the fortune onto the table, eating the cookie.

"How do they get the fortune in the cookie? It's like magic," I say.

"There's no such thing as magic," he says.

"Typical scientist. So cold and analytical. No imagination," my mom says, and gives me a look. "See what I had to grow up with?"

I definitely believe in science, like my grandfather does. But a small part of me is curious about magic.

Because cats.

There has to be something magical involved with creating them. The fluffy tails, the way they snuggle into loaf shapes and sleep in the sun. Most of all, the purring.

"What's your fortune say?" I ask my grandfather.

"Pfft," he says. "I'm not reading that thing. It's nonsense."

My mom plucks it up and reads it. Her eyebrows rise.

"Well?" he asks her.

"It says, 'You are going to be doing your own laundry.'"

Chicken Nuggets

The next morning, I'm ready to head out the door for school, but my grandfather is nowhere to be found. There isn't even a question of him not going to school. My mom's a teacher; she can't have truants in her own house. She's written a note to the middle school secretary explaining that "Ellie's cousin Melvin" has returned and will be attending again.

Finally, I find him digging through the large deep freezer in the garage.

"We don't have time to make burritos," I tell him.

"I'm not looking for burritos," he snaps. "I'm looking for my specimen!"

He shuffles some frozen peas. "Ah, there it is!" he exclaims, and pulls out the box. There's a packing slip with a note, and he reads it.

"Hmm," he says. "Billy thinks this is a jellyfish of some kind."

It was a secret formula created from a rare jellyfish that turned my grandfather young.

"We're going to miss the bus," I say.

"Fine," he says, and puts the box back in the freezer.

As we sit on the bus on the way to school, my grandfather stares out the window.

"Your mother's wrong, you know," he says abruptly.

"About what?"

I know she's wrong about a lot of things. Especially when it comes to making me turn off screens at night. Nine o'clock is way too early.

"What she said last night at dinner. About scientists being cold and analytical," my grandpa clarifies.

"They always make scientists look that way in movies," I say.

"Well, it's a ridiculous stereotype. Scientists are not robots! We're human! We feel things deeply!" he says. He shakes his head. "It's just that nobody understands us."

I know exactly what he means: grown-ups don't understand teenagers, either.

When we get to school, I drop my grandfather at the office so he can register. I'm heading to my first period when I run into Brianna. She's my old best friend from elementary school. We drifted apart when we started middle school. But it's strangely okay now. These days we're more like cousins who see each other at family reunions. We only remember the good times.

"You cut your hair!" she observes. "I like it!"

"Thanks," I say. She's always been good about that sort of thing: noticing.

She studies my hair. "You know, I think I still have this cute clip that would work for you."

When we were kids, we both had long hair. We shared ribbons and hair accessories and spent hours doing our hair.

"Really?"

She grins. "I'll bring it in tomorrow."

The bell rings and we walk away from each other, untwining like separate strands in a braid.

One thing has never changed since the first day of kindergarten: lunch can be either the best part of the day or the worst. This year hasn't been too bad. That's because of Raj.

Across the lunch court, he's holding a seat for me at our usual table. He slides a bag of barbecue chips to me when I sit down. We always share a bag at lunch; it's kind of our thing.

"Guess what?" I say. "My grandfather's home!"

He looks surprised. "Melvin's back?"

Raj is the only one besides my mother who knows the truth about my grandfather. Maybe that's another reason we're best friends. Who else could ever possibly understand me? It's like when people talk about being together during an earthquake. Only we know what happened when the ground started shaking.

"Yeah," I say. "He came home yesterday. He broke into the house because his key didn't work. I thought he was a criminal! The police came and everything!"

"Crazy," Raj says, and looks past my shoulder. "Oh, hey, here comes your criminal now."

I turn around to see my grandfather storming toward us with his tray, looking annoyed.

"Hey, Melvin," Raj says.

"Raj," he says. "Sticking rings in your nose is not very hygienic. You might want to brush up on germ theory one of these days."

My grandfather sits down and stares at his tray. He got the chicken nuggets.

"It's terrible!" he says.

"I wouldn't eat those chicken nuggets, either," Raj agrees. "They taste like Styrofoam."

"Not the nuggets. I've been held back!" my grandfather announces.

I'm confused. "From what?"

"Ninth grade! I was enrolled in eighth grade last time I was here, and they won't matriculate me. I have two PhDs, and now I have to repeat eighth grade for a third time? I'm going to have to read that infernal *Catcher in the Rye* again!"

"Should be an easy A, then," Raj tells him.

My grandfather glares at him.

"So," Raj says, "why did you come back?"

This is part of what I like about Raj: he's blunt in a nice sort of way. In middle school, everything anybody says has some hidden meaning. But I never have to guess with Raj.

My grandfather slumps a little. "I was tired of traveling. And I was sick of buses. You think the bathrooms are horrible here? You should try one on a moving bus."

"I bet," Raj says.

"And it was getting boring. My whole life, I've had a purpose. Working, science, and now . . . *nothing*. I don't know what to do with myself."

"So, you lost your mojo, huh?" Raj says.

"In a manner of speaking," my grandfather agrees. "Mostly, I miss my lab."

I imagine him wearing a white lab coat and standing at a stainless steel table, glass beaker in hand. It suddenly hits me.

"I have a great idea! You can be my partner!"

"In what?" he asks.

"The science fair. We can be a team and do a project together."

"A middle school science fair?" My grandfather makes a face. "I think I'm a bit beyond that, don't you?"

"But if you do the project with me, you'll get to be back in a science lab," I say. "It's brand-new."

He looks curious. "Brand-new, you say?"

"They redid the labs over the summer," I tell him. "I'm sure Mr. Ham would let us use his. He really wants kids to enter the science fair. What do you think?"

"I don't know," my grandfather says. He doesn't look convinced.

I think back to this morning and the freezer.

"We can do an experiment with that jellyfish in the freezer," I wheedle. "It'll be fun. Besides, you'll get to do science with me!"

He shrugs. "All right. How bad can it be?"

Then he takes a bite of the chicken nuggets and makes a face.

"Ugh," he says. "This is disgusting."

"Told you so," Raj says.

Doodle

Mr. Ham's science lab is my favorite room in the school because it's full of things kids aren't usually trusted to be around. Cabinets lined with glass beakers and test tubes. Big freestanding lab tables with water faucets and gas lines. Wobbly high stools that can tip over.

Mostly, I love the smell. It's not the usual school odor of pencils and dry-erase markers and boredom. It smells like chemicals and rubber and discovery.

"Ellie," Mr. Ham says with a smile. "How's your mom?"

Of course he knows my mom. It's a teacher thing.

"Good," I tell him.

"What's she staging this season?"

"*The Tempest.*"

"I love Shakespeare!" he says enthusiastically.

To be honest, Shakespeare kind of puts me to sleep. It's not Shakespeare's fault. My parents used to read his plays to me at bedtime when I was little, and now I associate Shakespeare with being tired.

"I'll definitely be buying a few tickets," Mr. Ham promises. "Now, what can I help you with?"

"I'm going to enter the science fair. With my cousin Melvin," I tell him.

"Wonderful! You and your cousin? Just like the Herschels," he muses.

"The Herschels?" I ask him.

"They were a brother-and-sister pair of scientists. Astronomers. You should look them up."

I nod. "Would it be okay for us to use the lab to work on our project? You know, after school."

He gives me a considering look. "Well, you *are* a

teacher's kid. I can trust you to use good judgment, right?"

"Of course. My mom would ground me for life if I got into trouble."

He laughs. "All right, you can use the lab while I'm next door grading papers. Just be sure to clean up after yourselves."

I promise him we will.

Like an animal freed from the zoo, my grandfather seems happy to be back in his natural habitat: the science lab. He prowls around, running his fingers along the tables, looking through cabinets, checking the equipment.

"This will do nicely," he says.

"What's our project going to be, anyway?" I ask him.

"I'm not sure," he says, putting the picnic cooler on a lab counter. That's how we brought the jellyfish to school. "It depends on the specimen."

He snaps on gloves and slices open the sealed plastic bag. A horrible smell wafts out of it: like sweaty gym clothes left in a locker.

"This is a very odd-looking jellyfish," my grandfather says.

"Why?" I ask. The defrosting pink blob in the middle of the pan has layers of tentacles.

He points to it. "Because it has legs. Jellyfish don't have legs."

He takes a pair of tweezers and gently lifts a tentacle. It falls off.

"Ahh, I see," he says. "This isn't a jellyfish at all."

"It isn't?"

"This creature was *caught* by a jellyfish. The tentacles were pulled off the jellyfish," he says.

"So the jellyfish killed it?"

"Not a very nice way to go, I'm afraid."

He hands me the tweezers.

"What am I supposed to do with these?"

"Remove the tentacles," he says. "This is a team project. I'm not doing all the work."

I pull off the tentacles, and it's strangely

satisfying in a gross way—like popping a pimple. The creature that's revealed looks like a cross between a fish and a salamander. It's got legs and a long tail.

"What is it?" I ask.

My grandfather studies it for a moment. "I believe it's an axolotl. Notice the gills."

"So it's a fish?"

He shakes his head. "Technically, it's a salamander, but it lives underwater. The axolotl has a very curious ability: it can regrow missing body parts."

"That's pretty handy," I say.

"Indeed. But I'm a little puzzled about something."

"What?"

"It has six legs. I'm fairly certain that axolotls have four legs. But I haven't seen one in many years. In any case, let's start documenting. Then we can head to the library and do some research."

He pulls a thick sketchbook and a pencil out of his backpack and starts sketching the blob.

"Why don't we just take pictures?" I ask. "We can use my cell phone."

"We didn't have camera phones in the old days. We learned by drawing."

"I'm not good at drawing," I tell him.

"It doesn't matter," he says. "Just doodle. Drawing helps you notice details. It makes you think."

So I do what he says: I doodle the blob. It's kind of fun. When I look over at my grandfather's drawing, I'm surprised. The lines are perfect and precise. It's amazing.

"Wow," I say. "You're really good!"

"Why are you so surprised?"

"Because you're a scientist."

He frowns. "I don't know where you get these ideas. Scientists are very artistic. You should see Van Leeuwenhoek's drawings."

"Van who?"

"Antonie van Leeuwenhoek, the creator of the first practical microscope. He drew what he saw. Bacteria. Protozoans. Blood cells. His drawings of fleas are beautiful."

38

Fleas are beautiful? I don't think Jonas would agree. He really hates flea medicine.

"I used to study those illustrations endlessly in college. They were so detailed," my grandfather says, his voice full of wonder. "You know, you can look at something a thousand times and then one day you see something new."

"Huh," I say.

My grandfather slaps his notebook shut. "Come on. Let's go get a snack. I'm starving!"

I gesture toward the stinky specimen on the tray. I feel nauseous. "You want to eat after this?" I ask him.

"This is nothing," he says. "Wait until you dissect a fetal pig in high school."

Ugh. Maybe Ben is onto something with the whole vegetarian thing after all.

When we get home, I break out my grandmother's recipe box. I like to cook, and I've been slowly working my way through it. There are a lot of recipes for casseroles and desserts I've never tried, like Bavarian Cream Cake and Noodle Pudding and something called Grasshopper Pie. Most of her recipes are simple, though. I decide to make her Best Banana Bread because we have all the ingredients in the house.

As the bread bakes, I hang out at the kitchen table surfing the internet. Jonas is sitting in the window, his nose twitching, waiting. The reason why appears a moment later: a fat orange tabby tomcat meows outside the window. It's Jonas's best buddy. The cat belongs to our neighbor. He keeps odd hours, and we've never met him.

Jonas jumps down and dashes out the cat door to play.

Speaking of buddies, I'm curious about my grandfather's blog. I expect it to be about science, but it's not. It's mostly just photographs of flowers. Hydrangeas and daylilies and daisies and wild roses. In some cases, he's written a little note, like a diary entry, next to the photo. One says, "The air smells like lemons." Another, "I miss snails." And then there's the cryptic note "Moss is underrated." I have no idea what they mean.

My grandfather's last blog post is a close-up photo of a dandelion by the side of a busy highway. It's a bright smudge of yellow with cars whizzing by in the background.

The diary entry says simply:

I see you everywhere.

My grandfather walks into the kitchen just as I've taken the pan out of the oven.

"What's cooking?" he asks.

"Banana bread."

"Your grandmother used to make the best banana bread," he says.

"It's her recipe," I tell him, slicing a piece. "Try it."

He takes a bite.

"Is it as good as Grandma's?"

My grandfather swallows. "Nothing will ever be as good as your grandmother's banana bread."

I feel a little let down.

Then he gives me a small smile. "But this is still delicious."

Genus and Species

"Why can't we just look it up on the internet at home tonight?" I ask my grandfather.

"The internet is full of false information," he insists. "Nothing is vetted. I trust books."

We're in the library. My grandfather is looking through various books for information on the axolotl. While I'm all for science, I'm also all for lunch. The only thing I had time to grab was a granola bar from a vending machine. I think of barbecue potato chips and Raj.

"Ah, here it is," my grandfather says, studying the book.

I look over his shoulder.

A photo that resembles our pink blob is on the page, only it looks more alive and cuter, with an almost cartoon-like expression. But the title under the picture says:

Ambystoma mexicanum

"I thought you said this was an axolotl," I say.

"That's its common name. *Ambystoma mexicanum* is its genus and species."

"Genus and what?"

"Genus and species are what scientists use to name living things. Genus is the category, and species is the classification. Naming is important. Without proper names, there's no order in the universe."

"Oh," I say.

"In any event, I believe our specimen is, in fact, an axolotl."

"But what about the extra legs?"

He shakes his head. "They could be either a genetic variation or an environmental variation."

He looks down at the page again.

"The most curious thing is that *A. mexicanum* isn't endemic to the Philippines," he adds. "This whole thing is a mystery."

"What's a mystery?" a voice asks.

My grandfather looks up, startled.

It's our new librarian, Mrs. Barrymore. She likes to wear bright retro fifties-style dresses with pop prints. Today, her dress has cherries on it. I'm not sure how old she is—late fifties or maybe early sixties? It's kind of hard to tell with old people sometimes.

"I'm helping my cousin do some research for science class," I tell her.

"I didn't know you had a cousin at the school, Ellie," she says.

"This is Melvin," I say. "Melvin, this is Mrs. Barrymore."

"It's my distinct pleasure to meet you," my grandfather says, extending his hand.

Mrs. Barrymore shakes it and smiles.

"Nice to meet you, too, Melvin," she says. "Do you need help?"

"I'm looking for more information on the axolotl. It's a species of salamander."

"Well, let's check the catalog and see what we can find."

"Thank you so much," he murmurs as they walk off together.

So much for lunch.

"Medium black coffee for Melvin!" the guy behind the counter shouts.

My grandfather grabs the steaming cup and starts drinking right away. I don't know any teenager who takes their coffee black. I always get a latte with extra foam and caramel and lots of sugar. Anything to mask the bitterness.

We've stopped at a sandwich shop near the

school to get a snack. After my sad granola bar lunch, I'm starving. I get a grilled cheese sandwich, and my grandfather gets a triple-decker turkey club, a side of fries, a frosted doughnut, a piece of coffee cake, and a bowl of chili. We take our food to a small table. There is a cheery little vase of flowers: blue carnations.

I watch my grandfather scarf down his food in short order.

"That's a lot of food," I point out.

"It's not my fault," he says. "It's the Puberty."

My grandfather says "the Puberty" like it's a disease.

I stare at the carnations. They make me think.

"What if the axolotl grew the extra legs because it ate something?" I ask. "You know, like how you use blue food coloring on flowers. The flower drinks it, and it turns the white petals blue."

"Go on," my grandfather says.

"Maybe our science project could be to figure out if the extra legs are from the environment."

"How do you propose we do that?"

"I guess we use the axolotl as food and see what happens."

My grandfather looks impressed. "Very nice. I like it. We'll need to pick up some supplies. We'll go tomorrow after school."

After we've finished eating, my grandfather pays up. As we're walking out the door, Brianna comes in. Her eyes widen when she sees my grandfather.

"Melvin!" she says. "I didn't know you were back."

"Do I know you?" he asks.

"You remember Brianna, right, Melvin?" I ask him.

He stares at her for a moment. "Is this the girl you went to kindergarten with?"

Brianna laughs. "Yes! Ellie and I were in the same kindergarten class! That's so cute that you know that!"

My grandfather turns to me. "Let's go."

Then he walks out the door.

"See you at school," I tell her, and give her an awkward wave.

My mom says Jonas acts like a teenager. He comes and goes as he pleases and sleeps all the time. Right now he's curled up between my mom and me on the couch on his fuzzy blanket. His eyes follow the action on the television screen.

"I think he's really part human," my mom observes.

We have an ongoing debate about Jonas's breed. His coat is thick and long, so I think he's got some Maine coon. My dad thinks he's part Siamese because he's so chatty. Ben swears he's a Norwegian forest cat.

"Maybe he's a new breed? *Feline humanus*," I say. Mom looks at me.

"Genus and species. The genus is feline and the species is human. Get it? It's science."

She shakes her head. "You and your grandfather are two peas in a pod." Then she adds, "At least your socks don't smell as bad as his."

His socks *are* pretty stinky.

"I wonder how Ben's going to deal with having him here," my mom says.

"He'll be fine with it."

But she looks a little worried. "I don't know. He already became an instant stepdad to you."

"So?"

"So you're easygoing," my mom says. "I keep waiting for your teenage angst to hit, but it hasn't so far."

"Grandpa's easygoing, too," I assure her.

My mom scoffs.

Just then my grandfather stomps into the den holding out a light-pink polo shirt.

"Look at this! It's pink!" he shouts.

"It certainly is, Dad," my mom says.

"It's supposed to be *white*." He looks pointedly at my mom and me. "*Somebody* left a red sock in the washing machine."

"Real men wear pink," my mom jokes.

He glares at her and then stomps out.

She turns to me and raises an eyebrow. "Easygoing?"

"It's probably because of his genus and species," I tell her. *"Teenage boyus."*

Mice Are Nice

Raj is late, so I'm holding our usual spot on the lunch court and freezing to death.

When I left the house this morning, it was warm and sunny, so I didn't bother to wear a jacket over my T-shirt. By the time lunch rolls around, it's cold and windy. I'm tempted to go fish something out of the Lost and Found box. But then I remember my third-grade teacher, Mrs. Bennett, and how she used to call it the Lice and Found box, and I think better of it.

Raj appears with a tray. "Sorry. I had to turn

in some work." He sits down and slides the potato chips to me.

"Thanks," I say.

"How's it going with Melvin?"

"Pretty good. We figured out the science project."

"You two should get matching lab coats."

Actually, *any* kind of coat sounds great to me right about now. I shiver when a gust of wind blows across the lunch court.

Raj frowns. He takes off his thick black leather jacket and hands it to me.

"I'm fine," I say, trying to wave it away.

"You don't look fine. You look freezing," he says, and pushes the jacket at me. "Besides, I'm wearing a fleece."

"Thanks," I murmur. I slip on his jacket. It feels like a warm hug.

"So, do you want to just meet me in the multi-purpose room after school?"

"After school?"

"The chess tournament. You're coming, right?"

In all the excitement with my grandfather, I totally forgot.

"We have to pick up supplies today for the science fair project," I say.

"No big deal," Raj says, but he sounds disappointed.

"When's the next one?"

"Week after next."

"I'll come to that one!" I tell him. "I promise I won't forget."

He gives me a small smile. "That works."

The bell rings and I hand him back his coat. I miss it already.

"Have fun with Melvin after school," he says. Then he makes a face. "Although I don't think 'fun' and 'Melvin' exactly go together."

I laugh.

After school, my grandfather and I catch a bus across town.

"I'm so sick of taking buses everywhere," he complains. "I miss having a car."

"You should be able to get your driver's license in a few years," I say.

"I suppose so." He looks wistfully out the window. "My first car was a beat-up used Chevrolet. What I really wanted was a Ford Thunderbird. In Aquatone Blue. It had a V-8 engine. Of course, there was no way I could afford that when I was a teenager."

The bus drops us off at a little strip mall. There's a thrift store. A doughnut shop. A pet store. A tattoo parlor.

"What are we doing here?" I ask. "I thought we were getting supplies."

"We are," my grandfather says.

I follow him into the pet store. It's quiet and dim inside. A man behind the counter looks up from his newspaper and waves.

"Let me know if you need any help," he says.

There aren't a lot of animals for sale; it's mostly pet supplies. Litter, food, flea treatments. The cat aisle has a nice selection of toys.

My grandfather strides past the snakes and frogs and heads straight to the back of the store. He stops in front of a glass enclosure full of mice. It has a sign that announces MICE ARE NICE!

Most of the mice are sleeping, curled up next to each other, their pink tails twitching. One lone mouse is darting around the cage, sniffing with his nose in the air, rubbing against the glass. My grandfather studies them.

"I think we should get five or so," he says.

I don't understand what he's talking about. "You want to get mice?"

"How else are we going to test your theory?" he asks. "We'll feed the axolotl to the mice."

My mouth drops open. "And then what?"

"We'll observe whether they're affected by it. I imagine we'll dissect them after—"

"Dissect them?"

I know he did experiments using mice when he was working as a scientist, but I can't imagine testing something on such a defenseless animal.

"I thought we were testing it on a plant or a flower," I say.

"Mice are standard test subjects," he says matter-of-factly.

"But it's wrong," I say. "They're so cute!"

"The cure for cancer may be discovered by experimenting on a 'cute' mouse one day."

The store clerk walks toward us.

"You want some help?" he calls. "The mice are on sale. Ten dollars each. I can give you a deal if you buy a few."

I shake my head at my grandfather.

Something crosses his face.

"Fine," he mutters. He turns to the clerk. "No, thank you."

"Thanks, Grandpa," I tell him.

"I guess we're going to have to do it the old-fashioned way," my grandfather says.

"Old-fashioned way?" I ask.

"We'll use *Drosophila melanogaster.*"

"What's that?" I'm worried it's the genus and

species name for something else cute, like a guinea pig or a hamster.

"Fruit flies. Do you have any deep feelings about them?"

I think for a moment. Does anyone have warm and fuzzy feelings about flies?

"I don't think so," I say, shaking my head slowly.

"Well, that's a relief." An excited look crosses his face. "Come to think of it, I haven't worked with fruit flies for years now. This is going to be a lot of fun!"

Then I remember what Raj said.

Only my grandfather would think fruit flies are fun.

We Are the Herschels

We get a starter pack of fruit flies from the pet store, but my grandfather tells me we're going to need a lot more.

"We'll have to breed them ourselves," he says.

"How?"

"We're going to make fruit fly media. The fruit flies will lay their eggs in it, and then the larvae will eat it."

"It's kind of like fruit fly baby food," I joke.

"In a manner of speaking," my grandfather agrees.

He makes a list of supplies for raising the fruit

flies. It's all basic stuff that you can get at a grocery store. The timing is perfect because our fridge is empty and we need to do a shop anyway.

"Make sure you get the ripest bananas you can find," he instructs me. "They're the key to the culture."

My mom and I like to go grocery shopping at night. There are no lines at the checkout, and people are usually happier. Probably because no one's rushing home to make dinner.

Tonight is no different. The aisles are deserted except for a random businessman staring at the single-serving-size dinners in the frozen-meals aisle.

I start filling our cart with things on my grand-father's list: oatmeal, yeast, confectioners' sugar, red wine vinegar, coffee filters. When we pass the barbecue chips in the snack section, I think of Raj and feel bad about the chess tournament. I grab a few bags of chips to make it up to him.

Then we're at the fresh fruit and vegetable

section. I head for the bananas and grab four of the brownest bunches I can find.

"By the way, I talked to your dad," my mom says. "He's going to be in town in a few weeks."

My father is an actor, and he's in the touring production of *Les Misérables*. I miss him a lot, but we text all the time. He's better at it than my mom; she has no idea how to use emojis.

"Great," I say as I put the bananas in the cart.

"Are you making more banana bread?" she asks.

"They're supplies for the science project Grandpa and I are working on," I explain. "For the science fair. I'll get extra credit."

My mom shakes her head.

"Speaking of extra credit, I could really use your help at the theater this weekend," she tells me. "The art department is way behind."

"I'll help out if you buy me the supplies," I bargain.

"Deal," she says.

"And some doughnuts, too," I add. "I'm

pretty sure there are powdered doughnuts in the experiment."

She rolls her eyes.

Mr. Ham is in the science lab when we arrive with our supplies the next day after school.

"So what are you two doing for your project?" he asks.

"We're breeding fruit flies!" I tell him.

"I like it," Mr. Ham says.

"And we're going to make our own media," my grandfather adds. "I have an excellent fruit fly culture media recipe."

"Very impressive," Mr. Ham says. "There's a blender in the cabinet you can use."

"Thank you," my grandfather says.

"I gotta run," Mr. Ham tells us. "Faculty meeting. Have fun whipping up the fruit fly media!"

We get out the blender, and my grandfather

hands me his recipe for the fruit fly media. I combine the bananas, confectioners' sugar, oatmeal, and vinegar and blend it to a soft consistency. It looks pretty good, actually, and I try it: it tastes a little bit like banana pudding.

"How long will it take for the fruit flies to grow?" I ask him.

"About two weeks," he says.

After the media is ready, my grandfather sets some glass jars on the lab table. He suggests that we put plain media in one jar and axolotl blended with media in another jar.

"Can we do a third jar?" I ask him.

"I don't see why not. What do you propose we add to it?"

"A chicken nugget."

"Why a chicken nugget?"

"I've always wondered what was in them," I say. "I saved one from lunch."

"Why not?" he says.

I hold the first jar while my grandfather pours

in the media mixture, filling the jar a quarter of the way. He sprinkles on some yeast, then takes a paper coffee filter and crumples it up and puts it on top. He shakes in some fruit flies from the starter container, puts a wet paper towel over the jar, and seals it with a rubber band.

I stare at the jar. The flies don't look right—they look like fleas.

"Something's wrong with our flies," I tell my grandfather. "They don't have wings."

"This strain of *Drosophila melanogaster* is wingless."

"Why?"

"Easier to study. They don't fly away. Also, they're what most pet shops carry. People use them to feed frogs, reptiles, birds. They're a very good live food source."

I feel bad for the flies. They don't have wings *and* they get eaten? It's like being stuck in middle school and then served up for lunch.

By the third jar, we've got it down. We make a good team.

"Have you heard of the Herschels?" I ask my grandfather. "Mr. Ham mentioned them to me."

My grandfather looks up and adjusts his glasses. "Of course."

"Can you tell me about them?"

"Caroline and William. William was the older sibling. He was an astronomer. He actually made his own telescopes."

"What about his sister?"

"Caroline was famous for discovering comets."

I wonder what their home life was like. Did William hang up his towel? Did he put the seat down on the toilet? Did he borrow his sister's zit cream?

"Did they share a bathroom?" I ask.

My grandfather looks momentarily puzzled.

"I don't believe there were bathrooms in the seventeen hundreds," he says.

"There weren't? Then what did they use?"

"Chamber pots," he says.

"What's a chamber pot?"

He gives me a weird look. "Why are you so curious about all this?"

"Because they were a family. Doing science."

He tilts his head.

"They looked at stars. We're making fruit flies," I say. "We're just like the Herschels."

He blinks. Then smiles.

"Yes," he says. "Yes, we are."

Shakespeare

In the Bay Area, people always talk about earth-quakes. We do earthquake drills at school and keep fresh batteries in our flashlights and bottled water in the garage.

My mom jokes that when the Big One hits, I'll sleep right through it. And she's probably right. Because these days, I could sleep all day. I didn't used to be this way. In fact, I used to be an early bird. But now it doesn't matter how early I go to bed; I can't seem to wake up. My mom says this is the true sign of being a teenager.

So it's no surprise that it's almost noon when I wake up on Saturday morning. Jonas is a warm lump under my duvet; only his pale-pink toes are visible. He loves to sleep. Maybe he's a teenager, too.

The house is quiet. My mom's already at the theater for rehearsals. I peek into the den and see my grandfather's hair sticking out from under the blanket on the couch.

When I walk into the kitchen, I spot the note my mom has taped on the dishwasher:

BROKEN. DO NOT USE!! THE SERVICEMAN HAS BEEN CALLED.

The theater is buzzing with energy when I arrive. There's a comforting feel to it because I know my way around this place: the catwalks, the wardrobe closet, the hot stage lights. I grew up here.

"You made it," my mom says. She's holding a clipboard. "Where's your grandfather?"

"He was tired," I say.

"Typical," she says. "Anyway, can you help in the art department, please? I really need that background flat to be finished today."

"Sure," I tell her.

I've seen *The Tempest* a few times. It's one of my mom's favorite plays to stage. She says it's the perfect Shakespeare play for high school because it's got everything: revenge, love, magic, family, and sword fights.

What I've always liked about the play is that it's not angsty. There's no blood and death like in *Macbeth* or *Hamlet*. There's no tragic romance like in *Romeo and Juliet*. Everything works out in *The Tempest*. People apologize for being mean. Families are reunited. Young lovers get married. It's all good feels.

And sometimes you need good feels, especially when you're in middle school.

The art department is working on a huge background flat of the opening scene: a storm at sea. Even though I'm not great at drawing, I love painting scenery. Someone else outlines it, and you just have to color in the lines. Sometimes I kind of wish life was like that.

As I paint, I watch my mom give the actors direction.

"The most important thing to remember is to get out of your head and *listen* to the other actors onstage. Acting is just like life: it's a collaboration. Not a solo effort."

Then they start the run-through.

My favorite character in the play has always been the old wizard, Prospero. Probably because he's bossy and reminds me of my grandfather. Unfortunately, the kid who's playing the part of Prospero is lousy; he doesn't know his lines.

After rehearsal, my mom and I stop at a pizza place to pick up dinner. We peruse the long list of toppings.

"How about mushrooms?" my mom asks me with a straight face.

"Very funny," I tell her.

We end up getting a pizza that's half mushroom, half plain, and a second pizza, with pepperoni, for my grandfather because he eats so much.

As we wait, Mom asks me, "What did you think of the kid playing Prospero?"

"He wasn't very good," I say.

My mom sighs. "They all want to be on Broadway, but they refuse to memorize their lines."

"Miranda and Ferdinand were great," I tell her. They're the young lovers in the play. "They look like they're really in love."

"That's because they are."

"Really!"

She nods. "They're dating. The stars in their eyes are real."

"How romantic!" I say.

"Until the production's over and they break up. Then it's gonna be tears."

"Maybe they won't break up. Maybe they're soul mates. Like Romeo and Juliet."

My mom gives me a look. "That didn't turn out so well, remember?"

"Oh, yeah," I say.

When we walk into the house with the pizzas, we hear banging. And then a loud curse.

My mom and I share a look.

"We picked up pizza, Dad!" my mom says, and then gasps.

My grandfather is sitting on the kitchen floor, surrounded by an open toolbox, screwdrivers, and scattered parts. The dishwasher has been pulled out and taken apart.

"What are you doing?" my mom shrieks.

"It should be perfectly obvious. I'm fixing the dishwasher," he says.

"But you don't know how to fix dishwashers!"

"I have two PhDs. I can figure it out," he insists.

"Like that time you figured out how to fix the dryer when I was in high school?" she scolds.

"It wasn't my fault! I didn't have the right part!"

As their shouting gets louder, I grab a slice of pizza and slip away to my room, with Jonas trailing after me.

Talk about drama. Even Shakespeare couldn't write his way out of this one.

Accidental Mold

I love horror movies. Especially the ones involving science. The experiments always seem to go wrong in Hollywood. Ants turn giant. Blobs take over towns. It's thrilling.

Our experiment is the complete opposite. The jars are full of fruit flies, and they look totally normal. I was hoping maybe they'd glow in the dark. Or turn into werewolves. (Were-flies?) I don't care, really; I just want *something* to happen.

I want a Happening.

Today when we go to the science lab after school, the flies look the same as always. Ordinary.

It's more like a Not Happening.

I make an annoyed sound.

"What's wrong with you?" my grandfather asks, looking up from his note-taking.

"This is so boring."

"Boring?"

"I was expecting something more exciting! A monster-movie situation."

"Hollywood always gets science wrong," he scoffs. "They want explosions and puffs of smoke!"

I kind of want that, too. Also, I'm a little concerned about something else.

"What about the science fair?" I ask him. "What are we even going to have to show?"

"What did you think would happen? What was your hypothesis?"

"Well, I figured the flies that ate the axolotl would change in some way."

He points to the jar. "What does the data show?"

"That nothing happened."

"So, what's your conclusion?"

"That this is a complete waste of time?"

He shakes his head. "The point of having a hypothesis is not to be right. It's about the data. Sometimes the data takes you in a direction you never imagined, and you have an interesting result. Like with penicillin."

"You mean the medicine? The stuff that tastes terrible?"

"That terrible-tasting stuff changed the world. Before penicillin, people died from simple infections. And its discovery was completely accidental."

"What do you mean?"

"Alexander Fleming was growing bacteria in petri dishes and didn't bother to clean them before he went on vacation. When he returned to his lab, the bacteria had been replaced by mold. The accidental mold—penicillin—had killed the bacteria."

This was kind of interesting. And gross.

"So penicillin is basically mold?" I ask.

"Yes," he says.

"No wonder it tastes so bad."

"Good scientists learn from their data." My grandfather taps his notebook. "Also, science takes time. You need to be patient."

I look at him.

"Okay," I say. "I'll try to be more patient."

He smiles approvingly. "Good."

"But I still want something to happen."

It turns out that my grandfather and Alexander Fleming have something in common: they're both messy. My grandfather leaves his dishes all over the place, and he doesn't pick up his socks. It's driving my mom nuts.

Everything comes to a head at breakfast on Saturday.

I'm experimenting with eggs and tofu. I usually make my scrambled eggs with ham or bacon, but since the vegetarian thing hit the house, meat is out. I figure I'll give tofu a shot, and I regret it immediately. The tofu falls apart in the pan, and the end result does not look appetizing. Even my grandfather won't touch it.

"What is that?" he asks, looking at the plate.

"Scrambled eggs with tofu," I say.

"I wouldn't feed that to a dog."

My mom marches into the kitchen holding a wet towel. "This has got to stop!"

"I couldn't agree more," my grandfather says. "I don't know how you people live without steak."

She shakes the towel at him. "You didn't hang up your towel!"

"Sorry," he says. "It must have slipped."

But I know by the look on my mom's face that she's just getting started.

"You're a pig. Even my college roommate was neater than you, and that's saying something!" She points to the den, where my grandfather's been sleeping.

The area next to the couch is out of control. There are piles of unfolded clothes, an apple crate filled with black socks, stacks of newspapers, a shoe box, crumpled tissues, dirty coffee mugs, empty water bottles, and towers of library books. Our house is small, so any clutter makes a difference. My mom and Ben talked about buying us a new house this year, but then real estate prices shot up.

My mother waves her hands. "Ben is coming home in a few days. You have to get this situation under control!"

"What do you expect me to do?" my grandfather asks, sounding like a grumpy teenager. "Maybe I'll just get a place of my own."

She props a hand on her hip. "Really? I'm sure a ton of landlords would love to rent to a fourteen-year-old."

I'm the one who helps avoid World War III by suggesting that my grandfather put his stuff in my closet. I have plenty of space. Also, I secretly love organizing things. I like order. Maybe it's the scientist part of me.

"Hey, look," I tell my grandfather. "I've organized my closet like genus and species. Genus *Pants*, species *leggings*, then species *shorts*. Funny, right?"

"Humph," he says, hanging up a shirt.

I stare at his side of the closet. He's hanging all the hangers backward. Not that there's a hard-and-fast rule on how to hang things, but I've spent enough time straightening the wardrobe closet for my mom's theater to know that you don't put the head of the hanger backward. You can't grab things easily.

"Why do you hang everything backward?" I ask him.

He looks at me. "This is the way your grandmother always hung things."

I didn't know that. But then, I don't know a lot.

My grandmother died when I was little, and my memories of her are fuzzy. I don't know if they're real or if they're just stories I've heard my mom tell. Some of the memories are sweet. Like how my grandmother always had a jar of pretzels in her kitchen for snacking. And some are odd. Like how she kept batteries in the refrigerator.

We manage to get all my grandfather's clothes into my closet and box up his other stuff. I clear a space on the top shelf for the boxes. I'm putting the last shoe box up there when I lose my grip and it falls out of my hand, the contents scattering everywhere.

"Sorry!" I say.

He sighs. "It's fine."

We start picking things up. There are old photos, a birth certificate, shiny buttons, programs, papers, and a lock of hair tied to a thin ring. But mostly there are books. Not the classics, either: old, yellowed paperback romance novels. Silhouette and Harlequin. The illustrations on the front covers feature couples staring at each other. I pick up one called *Captive of Fate.*

"Ah, yes," he says, "I remember that one quite well."

"You read this?"

"I've read all of them. Many times."

I'm a little stunned. I kind of assumed he read Einstein in his free time. Not pulpy romances.

"Really? They don't seem very, um, *you*."

"Your grandmother used to read them to me when I worked in the lab at night. It passed the time. Then when she died, I read them because it made me feel close to her."

It's strangely romantic.

"So, how do you like having Ben as a step-father?" my grandfather asks.

"He's great," I say.

It's true. Ben never tries to be my dad. He's more like a cool uncle. Also, he likes to play video games with me.

"I could never do that," my grandfather says.

"Do what?"

"Get remarried."

"Why not? Didn't you date after Grandma died?"

"Your grandmother was the only person I ever dated," he says, sounding offended.

"You never dated anyone else? Not even once?"

Not that I should talk. I haven't dated *anyone*.

"Why would I?"

"But aren't you lonely?"

He looks past me, an expression on his face I can't decipher.

"Of course I'm lonely. But I was destroyed when your grandmother died. You can't imagine what it was like to watch her waste away from the cancer. Two PhDs and a lifetime dedicated to science and I still couldn't stop a few malignant cells! I would have done anything to save her," he says fiercely. "Anything."

The room is quiet for a minute.

"I'm not going to go through that again," he says, and his voice sounds hollow.

"I'm sorry I brought it up," I tell him. I feel bad. He must have been so sad when she died.

"It's fine," he says, waving his hand, his face composed again.

He picks up a book called *The Burning Sands*. The cover features a handsome sheikh and a woman against a desert backdrop with camels.

"By the way, this one's my favorite."

"Why?" I ask him.

"Oh, that's easy," he says. "I've always wanted to ride a camel."

Games

When I walk out of my bedroom and down the hall, I see Ben's suitcase by the door.

"She lives!" my mom says when I walk into the kitchen. "We were about to send out a search party to see if you'd been abducted by aliens."

I join them at the table. My mom looks happy and Ben looks rumpled, his hair sticking out in weird places.

"What time did you get home?" I ask him.

"Around two in the morning," he says,

scratching his head. "I think? It's all a blur. Nothing like a twenty-one-hour flight to knock the stuffing out of you."

I'll never complain about the bus ride to school again.

"And I get to do it again in three days," he adds with a groan.

My mom smiles at him. "But it's all worth it, right?"

"Always," he says, and leans over and kisses her.

They're so mushy together.

"Isn't it a little early in the morning for *that*?" my grandfather grumbles as he comes into the kitchen still in his pajamas.

"It's noon," my mom says, smiling. Even my grandfather can't spoil her happiness.

"Good to see you, Melvin," Ben says. "Lissa mentioned that you're staying with us."

Ben thinks my grandfather is my cousin, because that's what my mom said the last time he lived with us.

"So it seems," my grandfather says, and blinks blearily. "I'm going back to bed. I'm exhausted." He leaves the kitchen.

My mom turns to Ben and makes a face. "Must be the Puberty."

Since Ben is home, we go out for a family dinner at a nice Italian restaurant. I avoid the mushrooms, of course. Afterward, Ben proposes we play a board game.

Ever since my mom married Ben, board games have been accumulating in our house. My mom jokes that he's really a big kid.

"No, thank you," my grandfather says. "I don't like games."

"Come on," I plead with him. "We can be a team!"

My mom grins. "I like it! Grown-ups versus teens."

"Grown-ups? Really?" my grandfather says to her.

She makes a face at him. "Come on, *kid*. Don't think you can beat me?"

"Please?" I beg him.

"Fine," he mutters. "But I refuse to play Risk. It takes too long, and Europe is completely indefensible."

We sit around the kitchen table playing a board game that involves castles and ghosts and giant spiders that eat you. It looks easy at first glance, but it's actually pretty difficult. At random points in the game, spiders kill you, and you have to go back to the beginning of the board.

"This is ridiculous!" my grandfather shouts when it happens to our team for the third time. "We have to start over *again*?"

My mom teases him. "But, Melvin, surely you've learned *something* from almost getting through the game already?"

I know she's not talking about the game.

But he ignores her and stares at the board. "I know from the math that we are taking the correct route to the dungeon."

"The math?" I ask.

"Yes," he says, tapping the board. "Board games are highly mathematical."

"It's true," Ben agrees. "I minored in math in college."

"What a waste of a college degree," my grandfather mutters beneath his breath.

"Not really," Ben says. "There's a lot involved in creating a good game. Storytelling. Math. Physics."

"Physics?" my grandfather asks.

"Yes," Ben says, and picks up the dice. "But *this* is the most essential thing to a game."

"Blue dice?" I ask.

"Chance," he clarifies. "It's the one variable that a player can't control."

Then he rolls. It's a five.

My mom counts the spaces and slams their piece into the dungeon.

"We won!" she cries.

Ben winks at me. "And it's also what makes games fun."

O   O   O

As far as games go, chess is a mystery to me. The only thing I know is that old men in the park like to play it. Do the players wear uniforms? Do you cheer? More important, are there snacks involved? In any event, I'm looking forward to seeing Raj play.

The multipurpose room is a whirl of activity. Players are lined up across from each other at long tables with chessboards between them.

Raj has his whole black-leather-goth thing going on as usual. But he's added something else that makes him stand out even more from the other kids: he's wearing sunglasses.

The girl he's playing doesn't look the way I pictured a chess player: she's got long blond hair and is wearing a sparkly sweatshirt with a unicorn. I'm starting to think Hollywood is to blame for all these bad stereotypes I have in my head.

Then it begins. And I'm surprised. Because the whole thing is exciting. Hands fly. Chess pieces are knocked over. Timers smacked. It's like the board game version of a contact sport. This is no joke.

Raj stares down at the board in concentration,

his hand jerking out to move pieces and hit the clock like lightning. He's focused and confident. He seems so much more than my potato chip–sharing friend. I remember what my grandfather said about looking at something a thousand times and then one day seeing something new.

Because it feels like I'm seeing Raj for the very first time.

Quiche

The next day at school, I chat with Raj at my locker.

"What'd you think of the chess meet?" he asks.

"It was pretty cool, but I couldn't really follow what was going on. I don't know how to play chess."

"I can teach you," he offers.

"Really?"

He smiles. "Sure."

We decide to do it the next day after school. He has to run a quick errand for his mom and then he'll come to my house.

When I get home from school that day, there's an unexpected visitor. But this time I don't call 911.

Because the criminal is so cute.

Lounging on our couch in the den is the fat orange tabby neighbor cat. He's curled up next to Jonas like he has a perfect right to be there.

"What are you doing inside?" I ask the orange tabby.

He blinks at me lazily.

"I'm pretty sure this isn't your house," I tell him.

My grandfather walks into the room. "You got another cat?"

"It's the neighbor's cat," I say. "He must have followed Jonas in through the cat door."

"Well, I hope he doesn't have fleas," my grandfather says.

"I thought you liked fleas," I say.

"Drawings of them," he clarifies.

I pick up the neighbor cat and carry him outside to his yard. He just looks at me.

"Go on home," I tell him.

Then I head back inside to the kitchen.

Since Raj is coming over to teach me chess, I want to cook something special. I decide on a quiche. It's easy to make, especially if I use a frozen piecrust. But our fridge is kind of empty: my mom's been really busy at the theater. There's no spinach or anything quiche-y. In the end, I use eggs, cheese, and . . . tofu.

I pop it into the oven. When the timer goes off, I put the quiche on the counter to cool, and in spite of the tofu, it looks delicious.

My grandfather comes into the kitchen, sniffing the air.

"What did you cook?" he asks.

"Quiche," I say.

"That will hit the spot nicely," he says, and picks up a knife. He goes to cut the quiche and I wave him away.

"Wait! Stop! You can't eat it!"

"Why not?"

"It's for Raj," I explain.

"The whole quiche?"

"No, of course not. You can have some later, after he gets here."

"But I'm hungry now," he grouses.

I shake my head.

"Fine. I guess I'll just have to walk to the convenience store and get myself a snack. May as well pick up a newspaper while I'm at it." He stomps out of the kitchen, muttering, "Enjoy your quiche!"

The doorbell rings, and when I open it, Raj is standing there with a wooden box. It looks like he just took a shower, because his hair isn't styled with mousse; there's a little curl to it.

"Brought my chess set," he says with a grin.

"Great," I say. "Come on in."

"Where's Melvin?" Raj asks as he follows me down the hall.

"He walked to the store to get a newspaper."

Jonas prowls up to Raj and rubs against his leg.

"Hey, Jonas," he says, scratching the cat's ears.

I tell Raj about the neighbor cat hanging out in our house. Raj thinks it's hilarious.

"He's been having cat parties while you're out?" Raj asks with a laugh. "How long do you think it's been going on?"

I wonder. "Hard to say. The cat's pretty comfortable here."

"It's like they've got this whole secret life that nobody even knows about."

We settle in at the kitchen table, and Raj sets up his chess set. He points out the pieces on the board.

"This big one is the king," he tells me. "The next biggest is the queen. Then there's rooks, bishops, knights, and pawns."

It reminds me of Shakespeare. His characters always seem to be court players.

Raj teaches me some basic moves, and then we take a break to eat. I slice up the quiche.

"This is good," Raj says.

But I've mostly been eating the crust. The egg part doesn't taste right to me.

"I don't know about this tofu," I confess. It's a little soggy.

"I'll eat it. Problem solved."

"We're pretty perfect," I say.

Something flashes across his face. "Perfect?"

"Yeah! You eat the eggy bit and I eat the crust. We're perfect quiche eaters!"

"Ellie," he says, and swallows. "I was wondering if you—"

Just then my grandfather rushes into the kitchen, his hand on his cheek.

"Ellie!" my grandfather shouts.

"Hey, Melvin," Raj says.

My grandfather ignores him.

"Does your mother have a dentist?" he demands, wincing.

"Why?" I ask. "What's wrong?"

"My tooth hurts! I bit a candy bar, and my crown fell off!"

He holds out his hand to reveal a big gold tooth-shaped crown.

"That's a lot of gold," Raj says with a low whistle.

"If I'd been eating quiche, this wouldn't have happened," my grandfather says, and scowls.

"I'll call Mom," I say.

It's weird how medical and dental offices are always so cheery. This one has smiling sea horses painted on the walls. Why are they smiling? There's nothing fun about getting a cavity filled.

"I swear," my mother says, "this is like having another child."

"At least you don't have to pay to send him to college," I tell her. "He's already got two degrees."

"Ha-ha," she says.

Ten minutes later, the dentist opens the door and calls us into the back. We huddle in the small exam room, where my grandfather is sitting on a dentist chair with one of those little paper aprons around his neck. He looks miserable.

"So, he's going to need the tooth pulled," Dr. Green announces.

"Pulled?" my mom says. She touches her own cheek.

The dentist pulls up an X-ray on her computer screen. She traces a gray line at the bottom of my grandfather's tooth. "The tooth is cracked. It was already a deep cavity with a crown."

My grandfather moans.

"By the way, where did he get his dental work done?"

"I'm not sure," my mom hedges.

"It's just that I haven't seen work like this on any patient younger than sixty," Dr. Green says.

She has no idea.

"By the way, I'm happy to give you a referral for an orthodontist. He's got a prominent overbite."

"I had an overbite, too," I say, thinking of the science. "Maybe it's genetic?"

My mom just sighs. "I can't believe someone else in this family needs braces."

"Braces?" my grandfather yelps.

A Happening

Back in elementary school, gym was fun. We played handball and foursquare. They let us use Hula-Hoops. But gym in middle school is terrible. The teachers are mean and the uniforms stink. Literally. No one takes them home to get washed.

Most of all, I hate running laps. They're boring, and I'm always one of the last kids to finish.

Today, we have to run a mile. It's pure torture.

"Hey, Ellie!" I hear a voice call.

I look back to see Brianna jogging up. She's like

my opposite: she plays volleyball for the travel team and is in really good shape.

She slows down to keep pace with me.

"How's it going?" she asks.

"Okay," I huff.

"Your cousin's in my math class," she says. "He's really smart! He finishes his tests before everybody."

I guess it helps to have two PhDs in middle school.

"What's new with you?" I ask.

"My dad wants me to go out for softball next year instead of volleyball."

She doesn't sound too happy about it. Her dad is pretty pushy. He's one of those dads who scream at coaches.

"I always liked your dad. He was so fun," she confides. "Remember that time he picked us up at ballet practice wearing his theater costume?"

He'd been running late and showed up dressed as the Phantom from *Phantom of the Opera*. My mom said the parents talked about him at pickup for years after that.

As we run laps, we reminisce about our childhood. It's easy talking to Brianna, comfortable. Like pulling on an old fuzzy sweater.

"Maybe we can hang out sometime?" she asks me as we finish the last lap.

I look at Brianna and see the little white scar on her forehead from when a kid smacked her with his lunchbox in first grade. I was there when it happened; I held her hand in the nurse's office when she cried. All these little moments that we shared that only we know. I've missed her.

But most of all, I've missed *remembering* with her.

"I'd really like that," I say.

The rest of the day passes in the usual blur of tests and taking notes and not enough time between classes. Finally, it's over and I head to the vending machines to get a granola bar.

Mr. Ham walks past me.

"Your flies are looking great, Ellie," he says. "Just be careful with them and don't let them escape and fly away. We had that happen a few years ago, and I've never heard the end of it from the custodian. It was a mess."

"No problem," I say automatically.

He walks off and I take a bite of the granola bar. What Mr. Ham said suddenly hits me and I start to choke.

Fly away?

I actually run to the science lab. And when I get there, I can't believe what I'm seeing.

Because in the jar that had the axolotl, the flies have . . . *wings*!

Talk about a Happening!

I stare at the jar in shock. Was this how Fleming felt when he saw the mold on his petri dish?

My grandfather walks in a moment later.

"I'm starving," he says. "Maybe we can stop by that pizza parlor on the way home today?"

"They have wings!" I tell him.

He makes a face. "I'm not a fan of hot wings. They give me indigestion."

"The *fruit flies* have wings!"

"But that's not possible," he says.

I point to the jar. "Look!"

He peers into the jar and his eyes widen.

"They have wings," he whispers.

"I know," I say.

He turns to me and grabs my shoulders, his face bursting with excitement. If he was a balloon, he would pop.

"They have wings!" he shouts.

"They have wings!" I echo.

We jump around like crazy people, laughing and shouting.

Until the door to the science lab opens. A teacher pokes her head in and we freeze.

"Everything okay in here? I was walking by and heard shouting . . . ," she says, her voice trailing off.

My grandfather and I share a look. He recovers first.

"Yeah, we're fine," he says. "Just raising fruit flies. It's very thrilling."

"Fruit flies? Interesting. Well, have fun. And keep it down."

The door shuts. There's a beat as my grandfather and I look at each other.

Then I say, "That was totally a Hollywood moment."

"Perhaps," he agrees.

My grandfather is eager to take a closer look at our flying fruit flies under the microscope. He picks up the jar of flies and walks out of the science lab.

"Wait! Where are you going?" I rush to catch up to him.

"The teachers' lounge."

"Why?"

"Because they probably have a refrigerator."

My grandfather walks into the teachers' lounge without any hesitation. I hover in the doorway as he heads straight to the refrigerator and sticks the jar of flies in the freezer section.

"What are you doing?" I demand.

"Cold is fruit fly anesthetic. They won't die. They'll just stop moving."

"Oh," I say. The room is empty, so I step inside and close the door quickly behind me.

After a bit, he takes them out. Nothing is moving.

Back in the lab, my grandfather shakes some fruit flies onto a petri dish and slides it under a microscope. He peers into the lens.

"Incredible," he murmurs.

"Can I have a look?" I ask, and he steps aside.

I do that weird wink thing and squint into the microscope. Most of the flies have wings. Not all of them, though. Some just have little stubs.

"I guess my hypothesis was right after all," I say.

"If our axolotl can grow wings on flies, it may be able to regrow other body parts! Organs, tissue, blood cells. Think of the scientific applications!" my grandfather says excitedly.

I don't know about the scientific applications, but I am sure of one thing.

"The fruit flies are waking up," I say, pointing to the petri dish, where wings are stirring.

We put them back into the jar.

Earthquake

"**G**ood news," my mom tells me. "Prospero is finally remembering his lines!"

"That's great," I tell her.

We're in her bedroom folding laundry. She has the biggest bed in the house, so it's easy to spread out. Jonas is curled up in a pile of towels still warm from the dryer.

She folds a shirt into a perfect square with a few quick movements. My mom is great at folding clothes; she worked at the Gap in high school.

"Anything exciting happening with you these days? I feel like I've been neglecting you with this play," she confesses.

I want to tell her about the winged fruit flies, but it feels like it's me and my grandfather's secret. We're like the cats who sneak into the house when the humans are away. No one knows what we're up to.

"Just hanging out with Grandpa," I say instead.

Jonas's tail twitches in his sleep as if he's dreaming.

"He's so cute," I say.

"Speaking of cute," my mother replies, waggling her eyebrows. "Are you interested in anyone?"

I hesitate. "Well, there is one boy I'm kind of interested in. . . ."

Her eyebrows rise. "Really? Who?"

"This boy right here!" I pluck Jonas out of the towels and hug him. He gives me an annoyed look and leaps out of my arms and runs out of the room.

"Very funny," my mom says.

But the truth is that ever since the chess meet, it feels like something has changed between Raj and me. I try to think of it scientifically.

What is the Hypothesis of Us?

We met, became friends, and then became best friends. But could we change into something more?

"Funny how your grandfather's dirty clothes always seem to mysteriously appear in our laundry." My mother holds out one of his polo shirts.

"He knows you'll end up washing them," I say.

"I don't know how my mother put up with him all those years," she says, shaking her head.

"Did you know Grandma liked romance novels?"

"That's right, she did. She always had a stack of them next to her bed." Mom looks at me curiously. "How did you know that?"

"Grandpa still has some of them," I tell her.

"Huh," she says.

"What kind of cancer did she have?" I ask.

"A bad one. Pancreatic. It moves fast." Mom looks down. "Although not fast enough in the end."

"What do you mean?"

"Her cancer was very advanced when it was discovered. Your grandfather wanted to try every last chemotherapy and radiation and experimental treatment under the sun, and I just wanted her to enjoy the little time she had left in her garden. She loved being outside with her flowers."

I remember my grandfather's blog. All the photos of flowers.

I see you everywhere.

My mom sighs. "It was a bad time for your grandfather and me. We fought a lot."

"What did Grandma want?"

My mom's face shuts down.

"I think she just wanted us to be happy. But no one was happy in the end. Because she died."

She shakes herself and gives me a lopsided smile. "Enough of this heavy talk. We have an important mission."

"Mission?"

She holds up the pile of my grandfather's clothes, a sneaky look on her face.

"We can't encourage bad laundry behavior! We need to 'lose' these clothes in a garbage bag with something stinky. I think that old cheese in the back of the fridge will work just fine."

I can't help but wonder who's really the teenager in this house.

The next day at lunch, Raj and I watch as my grandfather stuffs two pieces of pepperoni pizza into his mouth in less than five minutes. I don't think I've ever seen anybody eat so fast. Talk about a scientific achievement.

When the last bit of crust is gone, he stands up and burps.

"Are you getting more pizza?" I ask.

"I'm going to the library!"

"What's the rush?" Raj asks.

"I have research to do!"

Then he grabs his backpack and is gone.

"Wow, Melvin is on fire," Raj observes. "Guess he got his mojo back."

My grandfather is like a new person. He's literally got a spring to his step. He's excited and bouncy and constantly jotting things down in his notebook.

I'm starting to think that the wings aren't even the most important discovery. It's like my grandfather has found his old self again.

"Is this because of your science project?" Raj asks.

"Yeah," I say.

He shakes his head. Then he says, "There's a new horror movie opening on Friday."

"What's it about?"

"Zombies."

"Ooh," I say. I love a good zombie movie.

"I was wondering if you wanted to go see it," he says. His voice shakes a little. "You know, like a date."

It feels as if the ground moves beneath me, even though everything is still. This is an earthquake.

Raj is asking me out on a date!

I feel the same twinge of anxiety I felt when I debated getting the streak in my hair. Except this is way bigger than dyeing my hair.

"Just us?" I ask.

He looks momentarily unsure. "Uh, we could make it a group thing, I guess."

That sounds easier to me somehow.

"Let's do that," I say quickly.

"Okay," he says.

"What time's the movie?"

"Nine-twenty. Maybe we could go get something to eat before? There's a new restaurant near the theater. It's supposed to be pretty good."

"That sounds great," I say.

He cocks his head. "Who do you want to ask to come?"

I think for a moment.

"Leave it to me."

o   o   o

I ask Brianna in gym. We're stretching on the grass.

"That sounds like fun," she says. "Who else is coming?"

"Just me, you, and Raj so far," I say.

"We need one more person."

She's right, of course. Three is a weird number. My mom always hated playdates with three kids when I was little.

"What about Melvin?" Brianna suggests.

I groan inside. I know she has a little crush on him. But I really don't want to go on my first date with my grandfather.

"It's not really his thing . . . ," I start to say.

"He doesn't seem to have a lot of friends," she says. "It might be nice for him."

I say to myself: *How bad could he be? He's a grown-up, right?*

"Sure," I say.

The gym teacher blows her whistle. "Let's get going! Time to start laps!"

I groan.

"I'll run with you," Brianna says.

I give her a look. "Are you sure you want to go that slow?"

Brianna pulls me up and grins. "Come on."

Burgers and Malteds

"I thought we were just going to dinner?" my grandfather says.

We're taking the bus to the movie theater. I've never been on a bus this late at night. I feel like I'm breaking the law or something.

"Dinner," I tell him. "And then a movie."

I didn't exactly "ask" him if he wanted to go tonight. I explained that my mom has rehearsals at the theater and doesn't want me taking the bus by myself, which is why he has to come with me. I figured it was easier than asking him if he wanted to hang out with Raj and Brianna. I knew he'd come with me if I appealed to the whole safety aspect; he is my grandfather, after all.

The restaurant has a 1950s diner theme. There's a soda fountain counter. A jukebox blaring fifties music. And the waiters and waitresses look like they walked out of the wardrobe closet for *Grease*.

Brianna and Raj are already there when we arrive.

"Hi, Melvin!" Brianna says with a little wave.

My grandfather is polite. "Hello."

We're seated in a red vinyl booth with a Formica-topped table.

"This place is great!" Brianna says. "My family came here when it opened."

The waiter comes over to get our drink order. I look at the back of the menu. They have flavored sodas and milk shakes and something called malteds.

"What's a malted?" I ask.

My grandfather perks up. "They have malteds? I haven't had one in years! They're delicious."

"We make vanilla, chocolate, and strawberry malteds," the waiter helpfully suggests.

My grandfather's face lights up. "I'll have a chocolate one."

"Me too," I say.

"Me three?" Brianna says.

"Root beer for me, please," Raj says, and the waiter disappears.

Brianna leans forward. "The trailer for the movie is really good!"

"What's this picture about, anyway?" my grandfather asks.

"It's an end-of-the-world apocalyptic thing. Everyone turns into zombies," Raj says.

"Humph," my grandfather says. "Sounds like middle school."

Brianna bursts out laughing. "You're so funny, Melvin!"

The waiter reappears with our drinks.

My grandfather takes a sip of the malted, and a look of utter happiness crosses his face.

I try mine. It's like a milk shake, except thicker, and tastes like malted-milk balls.

"Can I take your dinner order?" the waiter asks.

"I'll have the veggie burger with everything," Raj says.

I haven't had a chance to look at the menu, so I order the same thing. I figure Ben would approve.

"Cheeseburger for me," Brianna says.

"How would you like it cooked?"

"Medium rare."

"And you, sir?" the waiter asks my grandfather.

"Hamburger with pickles and lettuce. Well done. Did you hear that? *Well done.*"

"Well done," the waiter repeats.

After the waiter leaves, my grandfather turns to Brianna.

"It's not a good idea to order food medium rare," he says.

"But that's how I've always ordered it," she tells him.

"Well, would you also like a nice case of salmonella? It'll make you vomit and give you diarrhea."

Brianna pales. But my grandfather's just getting started.

"Or how about listeria? That's an interesting

one, too. Fever. Convulsions. And you have a one-in-five chance of dying if you're diagnosed with it."

"I can die from a cheeseburger?" she asks.

This is *not* going how I'd hoped.

I hold up my cell phone. "Oh, um, Melvin. Mom texted. She needs you to call her back."

I drag him outside the restaurant.

"Give me the phone so I can call your mother," he says, holding out his hand.

"She didn't call!" I say. "You have to stop!"

"Stop what?"

"All the gross talk!"

"I'm a scientist. I'm just pointing out the facts," he says.

"Well, the fact is that you're ruining dinner!"

He frowns. "Fine. No more talk of vomiting or dia—"

I cut him off. "Grandpa! I mean it!"

As we walk in, he mutters under his breath, "Don't blame me if your friend dies a painful death."

120

o   o   o

My grandfather is more subdued when we get back to the table. Raj gives me a wink, and I know the date isn't ruined.

"So, Melvin," Brianna asks in a bright voice, "do you play a sport?"

"Do I look like I play a sport?" he asks.

"You look like a surfer," she says.

"It's your long hair," I tell him.

"I wouldn't waste my time with such nonsense."

Brianna tries again. "Well, what music do you like?"

He looks baffled for a moment. "The music that's playing now is excellent."

"I mean, is there a specific singer or band you like?"

"Andy Williams, I suppose," he finally says.

"Huh," Brianna says. "I don't know him."

She looks at her phone and does a quick search.

"Oh, wait! My grandmother listens to this guy. Isn't that old-people music?" she says, confused.

Raj chokes on his soda.

"It's not old," my grandfather insists. "It's classic!"

Brianna tries to engage my grandfather by asking him questions. What television shows does he watch? (None—they're a waste of time.) What apps does he have on his cell phone? (What's an app?) What cell phone does he like? (None—they're a waste of time.)

It's painful to watch. He's not rude exactly, but he makes it absolutely clear that they have absolutely nothing in common apart from being living organisms.

Finally, the waiter comes to the rescue with our food.

"How's your burger, Melvin?" Brianna asks.

"It's *very* well done, thank you," he says.

Then my grandfather looks around the restaurant. "I'd really like some more water. I hate how they never give you water these days unless you ask."

But it's busy, and our waiter just got started

with a big party. He passes by us twice and ignores my grandfather both times.

My grandfather stands up, holding his empty glass.

"Excuse me," he calls out loudly. "Can we have some water, please?"

I'm totally embarrassed and stare down at the table. Maybe the floor will swallow me up. Then I hear a glass shatter and look up.

A hush falls over the restaurant.

My grandfather stands there, clutching his stomach, an expression of agony on his face, the glass in shards at his feet.

"Melvin?" Brianna asks. "Are you okay?"

His eyes roll back.

And he crashes to the floor.

Emergency!

If you ever have to go to the emergency room, avoid doing it on a Friday night. It's like trying to get a seat at lunch when you're the last person in the lunch line, except with drunks and angry people who've been in fights. It's not a fun crowd.

Raj and I sit in the waiting room. Brianna went home, but Raj insisted on coming with me when the ambulance arrived. I'm grateful because I'm terrified and feel completely helpless.

"Maybe it was the hamburger?" Raj suggests.

"Do you think so?"

He looks mystified. "Maybe he was wrong about the whole well-done thing?"

My mom rushes through the doors of the emergency department.

"What happened?" she demands.

"I don't know," I say. "He just passed out in the restaurant."

A nurse brings us back into the curtained room. My grandfather is hooked up to wires and surrounded by beeping monitors. He'd woken up briefly after the fall in the restaurant but was groggy in the ambulance. Now he's asleep. With his eyes closed, it's easy to believe he's just a sick teenage boy.

A doctor wearing scrubs asks my mom questions.

"How old is your son?" he asks.

"My nephew," my mom corrects him. "And he's, um . . ."

"Fourteen," I say. "What's wrong with him?"

"Well," the doctor says, "it's looking like appendicitis. But we need to run some tests."

"Will he need surgery?" my mom asks.

"If it's appendicitis, he will. But let's not put the cart before the horse. I need a little more information. Does he have any medical issues?"

My mom looks momentarily bewildered.

"Um, I think he has high blood pressure," she says.

"That's a little unusual," the doctor says, and scribbles something down.

"And arthritis," she adds.

The doctor raises an eyebrow. "Rheumatoid arthritis?"

"I'm not sure."

"Anything else I should know about? Changes in diet?"

"He had a hamburger for dinner," I say.

"It was well done," Raj adds.

"Good to know," the doctor says. "We're going to get him admitted and will circle back to you when we have some more information."

O   O   O

A little after one in the morning, the doctor informs us that it's not appendicitis. But he wants to keep my grandfather overnight for observation, so they send us home.

My mom drops Raj off at his house.

"Thanks for staying with me," I tell him.

"No prob," he says. "Hope Melvin's okay."

"Me too. I'll text you tomorrow."

It's not until I crawl into bed that I realize we never even made it to the movie.

The pediatric ward is ridiculously cheerful. It's worse than the dentist's office. There are jungle animals painted on the walls—giraffes and rhinos and elephants. There's a play area with brightly colored furniture and an aquarium full of tropical fish. The nurses wear scrubs with flowers, and they have teddy bears on their stethoscopes.

I'm exhausted; I didn't sleep well at all. I

couldn't stop worrying about my grandfather. As we get closer to his room, the feeling in the pit of my stomach gets worse.

But then I hear him shouting.

"I'm starving! I didn't get to eat last night! Why can't I have solid food for breakfast?"

He's arguing with a nurse when we walk into his room.

"Jell-O is not breakfast!" my grandfather tells the nurse.

"This is what the attending physician ordered," he replies.

"I guess he's feeling better," my mom murmurs under her breath.

A doctor walks in; it's not the same guy as last night. He introduces himself and then turns to my mother, completely ignoring my grandfather.

"Well, we can't find anything wrong with Melvin. His vitals are good. The lab results came back negative for everything. So we recommend you bring him in for a follow-up at the clinic in a week. And, of course, feel free to call if anything changes."

"Excuse me! The patient is sitting right here," my grandfather says in annoyance.

"Sorry," the doctor says.

"So what caused this?" my mom asks.

"Most likely fatigue. It happens with teenagers. They run themselves down. We see it all the time. The abdominal pain was probably gas, since he'd just eaten."

"Well, that's a relief," my mom says.

"Why don't you go with the nurse and he can help you with the discharge paperwork?"

Everyone leaves the room, and then it's just me and my grandfather.

My grandfather scoffs at the closed door. "And he calls himself a doctor? He looks like he's barely out of college!"

"How do you really feel?" I ask him.

"Fantastic!"

It's all so crazy. "So it was just gas?"

"Of course it wasn't gas! It was my appendix!"

I'm completely confused. "But the doctor said it wasn't your appendix."

He taps his lower belly. "Trust me, it was my appendix."

"How do you know?"

"Because I haven't had an appendix since I was nineteen years old. And now I have one."

My mouth drops open. "But—but—how?"

"I injected some of the axolotl," he says.

"You did what?"

"Well, I assumed that since the fruit flies grew wings, the axolotl would grow back my missing tooth. But instead, it grew an appendix! Talk about an interesting result!"

I can't believe it.

"What's wrong with you? That was dangerous!"

He looks unconcerned. "Scientists take risks! Besides, I figured I had a fifty-fifty chance, like Carroll and Lazear."

"Like who?"

"James Carroll and Jesse Lazear. Two doctors who allowed themselves to be inoculated by mosquitoes infected with yellow fever. At the time, they were trying to figure out if yellow fever was spread by mosquitoes."

"What happened?"

"They both got yellow fever, of course."

"So they proved it?"

"Yes," he says. "And Jesse Lazear died."

I gasp. "He died?"

My grandfather's brows furrow. "Of course he died! It was a fatal disease at the time. That's why he was trying to figure out how it was spread."

"What is wrong with you? What if you'd died?"

He waves me off. "It all worked out. Now, can you please go down to the cafeteria and get me something decent to eat? Pancakes or an egg sandwich?"

As I walk toward the door feeling dazed, he shouts after me.

"I'll take waffles, too, if they have them! And bacon!"

Horror Movie

"I saw Melvin between classes," Raj says. "He looks okay."

"Yeah," I say. "He's fine now."

Although he did milk the whole hospital thing a little bit. He spent the rest of the weekend lying on the couch, saying he was exhausted. My mom even did his laundry for him. Maybe he should have gone into theater after all.

"I can't believe it was just gas," Raj says. "He looked like he was in so much pain."

I want to say that's because he was growing a brand-new appendix, but I don't.

Raj looks around the lunch court. "Where is he, anyway?"

"The library, probably."

"He sure spends a lot of time there," Raj observes. "You think he has a crush on Mrs. Barrymore?"

I laugh. "No way."

"She's near his real age," Raj points out.

Which is true. But I can't really see the crush part. My grandfather didn't seem as if he was over my grandmother.

"Anyway, I heard the movie was great," Raj says.

"It figures," I say.

"Do you want to try again to see it?" he asks.

If Raj was cast in the play of my life, he'd be the hero. Not just because he's tall, goth, and handsome. But because he's loyal. He stayed by my side in that horrible emergency room when I was scared.

"I'd love that," I say.

"Maybe this time it should be just us?" Raj suggests.

That sounds good to me.

My mom likes to stalk the racks of thrift shops for costumes for her plays. Sometimes she brings home stuff for me, too. Puffy blouses, bright vinyl belts, seventies-style skirts. They're almost always too loud or too odd for me. I'm all about comfort: I like soft, I like fuzzy, and I hate anything too tight.

But when Friday night finally arrives, I find myself staring into my closet. For some reason I want to look *interesting* tonight. I decide to wear one of the thrift store finds: a silky shirt with a loose bow tie. It looks casual and dressed up at the same time. Like I'm not trying too hard, even though I am.

"You look lovely," my mom says. "I knew that shirt was perfect for you."

Ananda, Raj's college-age brother, is home from

school and drives us. He's not a big talker. I once asked him why.

"Because somebody has to listen," he told me.

Even though Ananda is quiet, the car is full of the sound of Raj and me chatting.

"Let's make a bet," Raj says. "Who's going to survive the film: humans or zombies?"

"Team Zombie," I say. I always stand with the monsters; they're totally misunderstood.

"Okay, I'll take the humans. What are we betting?"

That's easy. "Barbecue chips for a week."

Raj grins. "Nice one."

We pull up at the multiplex.

"We'll meet you out front after," Raj tells his brother as we get out of the car. Ananda just nods.

Raj already has tickets, so we don't have to wait in line. Inside, we get a big tub of popcorn (extra salt) and two sodas (root beer).

The poster outside our theater says BE PREPARED TO BE TERRIFIED!

"Are you prepared to be terrified?" Raj jokes.

"Bring it," I say.

Then we step into the dark.

Part of the reason I love horror movies is that they don't scare me. I grew up around stage makeup and fog machines. I know how to make fake blood and how to fall down dead onstage. Everything's an illusion.

But this movie is actually terrifying. Although it has nothing to do with what's happening on the screen.

Raj is holding my hand.

And it feels . . . *weird.*

I don't know what to do. I'm right-handed, so how do I pick up my soda? What if I have to go to the bathroom? Also, his hand is kind of sweaty. I don't remember Shakespeare mentioning this in any of his plays.

Halfway through the movie, Raj lets go of my hand and takes a sip of root beer.

And I'm relieved, which is confusing. What's wrong with me? Shouldn't I want him to hold my hand?

I keep my eyes fixed on the screen, waiting for him to take my hand again.

But he doesn't.

I know I should be the one to take his hand.

But I don't.

After the movie, we wait outside on a bench for Ananda to pick us up.

"So, uh, that movie was really good," Raj says.

It was terrible. The zombie makeup wasn't very scary. And why do the humans always hide in the basement? That's the first place I'd look if I was a zombie.

"Yeah," I agree.

We're like people from a different country. We don't understand each other. We don't speak the same language anymore.

On the drive home, the car is quiet. It's awkward. Even Ananda senses it.

"So, uh, how was the movie?" he asks.

I know things are really bad if Ananda is actually talking.

"Great," I say.

"Great," Raj echoes.

We pull up to my house.

"Thanks for the ride," I say politely.

"See you tomorrow," Raj says.

Real-Life Zombies

I don't see Raj the next day at school. Because I avoid him.

And he avoids me.

If we pass between classes, we stare straight ahead, never acknowledging each other.

It's as if we've turned into real-life zombies.

The worst part about all of this friends-maybe-more-maybe-not awkwardness is that Raj is the one I would usually talk to when I'm upset. But now I can't. Because we're not talking.

Instead of going to the lunch court, I grab a

granola bar from the vending machine and go to the science lab. I pretend I'm working on my science project so I don't have to see Raj. The fruit flies with wings seem a little sluggish, like they're depressed. I feel their pain.

This is what my life has come to: hanging out with fruit flies.

Mr. Ham is usually next door grading papers when I'm in the lab, but today he's here.

"That doesn't look very filling," he says, eyeing my granola bar.

"It's not," I admit.

He has a huge piece of lasagna. It looks delicious.

"Here," he says, and cuts his lasagna in half. "Have some."

"Thanks," I tell him.

We eat for a few minutes. The lasagna is amazing. It's got chicken and spinach and is smothered in cheese.

"So, I bought advance tickets for *The Tempest*," he says.

"My mom will be really happy," I say. It's hard

to get a sold-out show in high school. Sometimes she makes her students go to the show as part of their grade.

"It's funny," he says. "I wanted to go into theater when I was in college."

"Really? Why didn't you?"

He looks thoughtful. "I asked too many questions. Why was the director using a single spotlight? Why was the art department using fake trees when we could have bought a real ficus? I drove everyone nuts."

I could see that. Even though a play is a collaboration, it will fall apart with too many captains.

"About that time, I really got into science, and I knew it was for me. Because science is all about asking questions."

"I like that about science, too," I say.

The bell rings and I stand up.

"Well, thanks for lunch. It was really good," I tell him.

"It was a new recipe I've been playing around

with. The portobello mushrooms work much better than tofu."

My mouth drops open. "Mushrooms?"

"Yes," he tells me. "The big chunks you ate? Those were mushrooms."

I'm completely bewildered. The lasagna didn't taste like mushrooms; it tasted *delicious.*

"I thought it was chicken," I say.

"Oh, no." He laughs. "I'm trying to be vegetarian these days."

Who isn't?

After a few days, the science lab gets old. I follow in my grandfather's footsteps and go to the library at lunchtime. The library has a smattering of students, most of them working on the computers. I expect to see my grandfather doing the same thing but instead discover him shelving books with Mrs. Barrymore. I find myself creeping up behind one of the tall bookcases to eavesdrop.

"Now, *this* was a good movie," he says, holding up a book. I see the title: *To Kill a Mockingbird*.

"Gregory Peck will always be Atticus Finch to me. My late husband loved that movie," Mrs. Barrymore says fondly.

My grandfather looks curious. "So, why haven't you remarried?"

Most grown-ups would probably say something like "That's kind of personal" or "None of your business," but Mrs. Barrymore answers him.

"To be honest, I've needed some time to get over my husband's death."

"Yes, I can see that," he says.

"He'd been sick for a long time. He had Parkinson's," Mrs. Barrymore says. "It was hard."

I may not have two PhDs, but even I can tell from her voice that it was worse than hard.

Then my grandfather says, "When my . . . *grandmother* died from cancer, my grandfather had a hard time moving on. He said he felt lost."

Mrs. Barrymore sighs and looks a little sad. "I know exactly what he meant. I kept my husband's

143

toothbrush in our bathroom for a long time. Isn't that silly?"

"It doesn't sound silly to me."

"How is your grandfather now?" Mrs. Barrymore asks.

He answers carefully. "I think he's a little lonely."

"I feel the same way," she says.

Even though I packed my lunch the night before, I forget to bring it to school in the morning rush. I can't bear the thought of eating another vending-machine granola bar, so I break down and go to the lunch court.

Once I have my tray, I don't know where to sit. Raj isn't at our usual spot—some kids I don't know have camped out at it. In fact, I don't see Raj at all.

But I do see Brianna. She's sitting by herself, scrolling through her phone. I head to her table.

"Can I sit here?" I ask.

She smiles widely. "Ellie! Of course!"

The hot lunch today is chicken nuggets. I take a bite. They're hard and cold. "Yuck."

"Not as good as crispy corn dogs?" she teases.

We had a crispy corn dog inside joke when we were younger.

"So that dinner was pretty crazy, huh?" she says. "I thought Melvin was dying or something."

"Just really bad gas," I tell her.

"He's not into me, right?" she asks.

"It's not personal. He's not interested in anybody."

Brianna shakes her head and sighs.

We sit quietly for a moment and watch the action on the lunch court like it's a movie. There's a tall, thin boy balancing a tray in one hand and a phone in the other. He stares at his phone as he navigates the crowd. Or doesn't. Because he walks right into another kid, knocking his tray to the ground. The food splatters everywhere.

Brianna and I can't help ourselves: we crack up laughing. It's terrible. But a kid dropping food never gets old.

"I thought he was kind of cute until he dropped the tray," Brianna says.

"Raj and I went on a date," I say suddenly.

She looks at me.

"I figured you liked him," she says.

"It's all a mess, though," I tell her.

"Why? What happened?"

"That's just it. Nothing really happened. We went to a movie and now we're not talking. It just felt weird."

"Oh," she says sympathetically. "That's too bad."

I realize what else is weird: I'm talking to my old best friend about my new best friend, who I'm not talking to at the moment.

"Sometimes I miss being in elementary school," Brianna confesses. "Everything was easier."

I know exactly what she means.

"Remember kindergarten?" I ask. "We didn't even have homework! All we did was play and eat animal crackers."

"Animal crackers were the best! Why don't we eat them anymore?"

"I don't know," I say. "I guess it's some dumb rule. No animal crackers when you grow up."

She grins at me. "You know what? I'm going to bring some animal crackers for us tomorrow."

"Think they'll taste the same?"

Brianna points to my tray of chicken nuggets. "Anything will taste better than that."

And we both laugh.

Bad Dream

I might be able to sleep through an earthquake, but apparently I can't sleep through a cat meowing.

The sound pulls me right out of a dream. It was a weird one, anyway. I dreamt I was at school and I was wandering around an empty lunch court. I couldn't decide where to sit, and I was so lonely. Maybe it was actually a nightmare.

I look around and see Jonas sitting by my closed bedroom door.

"Do you want to get out?" I ask him, and then

realize he's not the one making all the noise. The meowing is coming from the *other* side of the door.

I open the door and reveal the culprit: the orange tabby.

"Isn't it a little early for this?" I ask the cat.

The cat doesn't seem to care; he brushes up against my bare leg.

"This isn't your house, you know," I say as I walk to the kitchen, the two cats trailing behind me.

I give Jonas his morning wet food, and the orange cat watches as he eats. I feel a little guilty about not giving the other cat any food, but I think he'll probably just move in if I do.

"I have to go to school. What are you guys going to do today?" I ask them.

The orange tabby cat turns tail and makes a run for the cat door, and Jonas darts after him. They slip outside.

"I guess that's my answer."

O   O   O

The bus is packed after school. And naturally, the only empty seat is next to Raj. I guess the whole goth thing can be kind of intimidating.

When I walk past him, I pretend I don't see the seat. I don't stop until I reach the back of the bus. Of course, my grandfather is only too happy to grab the empty seat.

I hold on to the pole and watch them as they talk. My grandfather waves his hands as Raj listens. What's going on? What are they talking about? What am I missing? I feel completely left out.

The two of them chat until Raj gets off.

Finally, it's our stop, and my grandfather and I get off the bus and walk home.

"So, Raj told me he's made it to the finals in the chess competition," my grandfather says. "I'm impressed, even if he does insist on putting holes in his nose."

I shrug but don't say anything. I can't believe he knows more about Raj than I do.

"What's going on with you?" my grandfather asks me.

"Nothing," I say.

"Is this the Puberty?"

"It's not the Puberty! I don't want to talk about it."

He studies me for a moment.

"Fine," he says, and it's silence the rest of the way home.

Jonas is lying in the sun on the bottom porch step when we walk up the driveway. The orange tabby tom is next to Jonas, grooming him.

"What adventures have you boys been up to today?" I ask them.

Jonas blinks at me.

"Come inside and I'll give both of you a snack."

I unlock the front door and open it. The orange tabby cat darts inside.

My grandfather is staring at Jonas, an odd expression on his face.

"Come on, Jonas," I say.

At the sound of my voice, Jonas lifts his head. His front paws scramble and he tries to drag himself up the step, but his hind legs just lie there. He gives me a confused, tired look.

My grandfather goes still.

"Ellie," he says in an urgent voice. "Call your mother."

The receptionist comes around the desk and shouts for a veterinarian when we walk in the door of the animal hospital carrying Jonas wrapped in a towel. They take him to the back right away.

My mother and grandfather and I sit in the waiting room with other pet owners and their animals. The waiting room is over-the-top cutesy with posters of playful puppies and baskets of kittens. The whole thing has a horrible feeling of déjà vu. This is like the animal version of my grandfather's visit to the emergency room.

Finally, they let us go back to see Jonas. The examination room has that same antiseptic smell as the hospital. My cat is lying on a stainless steel table with an IV, and he doesn't even look up when we come in.

The veterinarian is wearing scrubs decorated with puppies.

"He's in shock, and there are neurological issues," she tells us. "When did you last see him?"

"This morning," I say. "He was fine this morning!"

"He may have fallen from a high floor," the doctor says.

"We live in a one-story house," my mom says tearfully.

"And we have a cat door!" I add.

The doctor looks thoughtful. "Then he was most likely hit by a car. We see this sort of thing a lot when animals experience traumatic injuries."

My mom squeezes my hand.

The veterinarian gives Jonas a considering look.

"He definitely has some paralysis in his back legs, so we need to run some more tests. We'll give you a call after the tests are finished, and we can assess next steps then."

On the drive home, I stare out the window. How

did this happen? Everything changed in the blink of an eye.

My mom tries to be optimistic.

"That vet seemed very smart," she says. "I feel like Jonas is in good hands."

But my grandfather, who always has an opinion, says nothing.

Anything

The next day at school, everything is a fog. I go through the motions, but I don't pay attention. How can I possibly care about math when Jonas is hurt? I hold it together until I get to last period, science. And then I see Mr. Ham's tie: it has cats on it.

I go to the bathroom and throw up.

Mr. Ham sends me to the school nurse, who lets me lie on the couch-bed and gives me some water. I tell her what happened and she's sympathetic. She works weekends at the emergency room.

"Sometimes these things turn around," she says. "Don't give up just yet."

Part of me is still hopeful when we go to the animal hospital after school. But when I see the look on the vet's face, that hope is smashed, and all the glue in the world can't put it back together.

"I'm so sorry," the vet says. "I'm afraid it doesn't look good."

"His spinal cord?" my grandfather asks, and he sounds like a doctor.

"Yes," she says.

"I suspected as much," my grandfather murmurs.

My mom's breath hitches on a sob.

"Can I see him?" I whisper.

"Of course," the vet says.

Jonas is lying in a padded cage, his eyes closed. He doesn't even look like he's breathing. He's got an IV in his paw.

"How long?" my mom asks.

"It's hard to say. In a case like this, he may linger a day or two," the vet says. "Or we can put him to sleep."

"I don't understand!" I say.

The doctor gives me a practiced look. "We can manage his pain and hydrate him, but he's not going to improve. His spinal cord is badly damaged."

My mom makes a small sound. She looks like she's going to start crying.

"What about antibiotics?" I ask. "Like penicillin?"

The doctor just looks at me.

This is all happening too fast. I can't take it in.

"You want to put him to sleep?" I burst out. I look at Jonas. "He's a fighter. I know he is!"

"We'll have to discuss it," my mom says.

Then the doctor says in a terribly kind voice, "Take all the time you need."

My mom drops my grandfather and me off at home. She has dress rehearsal tonight, so she has to go back to school, especially after canceling last night.

"This is awful timing all around," she says.

157

I nod like I understand. But I don't. How can there be a good time for something like this?

My mother says, "We'll make a decision in the morning. I'll call and check on you."

Then it's just me and my grandfather. I'm full of nervous energy. I can't bear to sit still; I need to be busy.

"I'm going to make dinner," I say.

"Good idea," my grandfather replies.

The kitchen is a mess. It's been completely neglected in the last twenty-four hours. I unload the dishwasher, scrub the dirty pots and pans, and wipe down the counter. The cleaner the kitchen gets, the calmer I feel.

Then I pull the overflowing trash bag out of the container and carry it to the garage. My eyes fall on the deep freezer in the corner, and suddenly it's so obvious.

My grandfather's sitting on the couch when I walk into the den.

"The axolotl," I say.

He sighs heavily as if he's been waiting for me to say this.

158

"It grew wings and an appendix. Would it regrow a spine?"

"I don't know," he admits.

But I *do* know.

"Please!"

"Ellie," he cautions me. "You need to think about this very carefully. There's no guarantee it will work. And it may actually hurt Jonas. Animals can't tell us when they're in pain."

I flinch at the thought of Jonas suffering. But I don't know what to do. Should we try—and maybe cause Jonas pain—in the hope that he'll live? Or do we just let Jonas live out his last days and then let him die? I suddenly understand better what my grandfather and mother went through with my grandmother, because these are impossible choices. Everything is horrible.

Then I look at the couch, at the empty fuzzy blanket, and imagine my cat curled up there. I know in my heart that I can't just let him die without trying. So I say the words I know will sway my grandfather.

"I would do *anything* to save Jonas," I say.

My grandfather closes his eyes and nods.

We take a cab to the animal hospital, and my grandfather does the talking when we get there. He explains that we want to take Jonas for one last night at home and that my mom is waiting outside for us in the car. The vet doesn't seem the least bit surprised.

"A lot of people do this," she tells us. "I always encourage it. It's a chance to say good-bye."

Then we're back in the cab, this time with my cat. My feelings waver between worry and hope.

"It's going to be okay," I tell Jonas.

At home, I take Jonas out of his cage and put him on a pile of towels with his favorite blanket from the couch on top. He looks confused but doesn't even twitch when my grandfather injects the axolotl through a syringe into the base of his spine.

After it's over, my grandfather orders Chinese

food for dinner. I'm actually hungry for the first time since all this started. I try to feed Jonas a little chicken, but he ignores it.

My mom calls to check in on us, and my grandfather tells her everything's fine. We move into the den and sit on the couch with Jonas on the blanket and watch TV. The lawyer show is comforting because I don't have to pay attention to know what's going on.

An owl hoots somewhere outside, the sound carrying through the open window.

For the first time, Jonas lifts his head.

"Is it okay to take him outside?" I ask my grandfather.

"It's fine," he assures me.

We sit with Jonas on the deck. It's a clear night, the sky a blanket of stars.

"Is that a comet?" I ask, pointing up at a light moving fast across the sky.

"It's moving too fast. That's probably a satellite. Also, comets have tails."

"Like cats," I say.

We don't say anything for a minute. My cat seems content to be outside and looks around at every noise.

Then my grandfather says abruptly, "She called it 'minding the heavens.'"

"Who did?" I ask.

"Caroline Herschel called her observations of the night sky 'minding the heavens.' I always liked the sound of that phrase."

I see what he means. It makes something scientific sound almost magical.

"I like it, too," I say.

The three of us sit there until my mother comes home, the soft night air around us as we mind the heavens.

Time

When I wake up, bright streaks of light are spill-ing around the edges of my blinds, giving my room a warm glow. It's morning. The sun is shining. A fresh day. I feel hopeful. Then I look down at the floor and see Jonas.

He's breathing funny. Panting. Like a dog.

I go over to him and say, "Jonas, what's wrong?"

But he just pants, his mouth open, his pink tongue sticking out, and I know this isn't right.

"Grandpa!" I shout.

My grandfather is there a moment later. He's already dressed for school.

"Ellie?"

"Something's wrong with Jonas!"

My grandfather gently rubs the side of my cat's belly.

"He's in respiratory distress," he says. "It happens with spinal injuries."

"So it didn't work?"

He strokes his hand gently along the back of Jonas's spine near the tail and then touches the bottom of a back paw. My cat doesn't move. The whole back of Jonas's body is limp as a rag.

My grandfather looks at me, and although his face is young, his eyes are old.

"Ellie," he says, "there was too much damage to his spine."

"Can't we just give it more time?" I ask desperately.

"Time can't fix this," he says. "I'm sorry."

I look at Jonas panting.

And I'm sorry, too.

o   o   o

Everyone is very helpful. The receptionist helps my mother fill out the paperwork, and the assistant brings me tissues. The vet comes out and asks if we have any questions about what's going to happen.

But the questions I have, no one can answer: Why is my cat dying? How can everybody be so calm about it?

They bring us into the little examination room. There's a tray with shots. Someone's put a thick plush blanket on the stainless steel table. Jonas is already lying there, his eyes shut.

"Hi, Jonas," I whisper, but he doesn't seem to hear me.

"Do you want to stay with him?" the vet asks me.

I look at Jonas lying there and then at the vet. I'm not brave like those scientists who infected themselves with the yellow fever virus. I'm a complete coward. I shake my head.

"It's all right. I'll stay," my grandfather says in a gruff voice.

"We both will," my mother adds.

My grandfather looks at her and then nods.

"Go wait outside, sweetie," my mom tells me.

I rush out of the room without looking back.

My grandfather croons to Jonas, "It'll be okay, old fella."

For once, I don't hope for a Happening. I want everything to be boring and normal again. I wish I was in school. I'd be in second-period math, and I'd be so happy to take a test right about now. I would give anything not to be sitting here pretending to read old magazines.

I want time to slow down, to reverse, to go backward. But the clock on the wall is cruel. The minutes tick by—one, two, three, four. Before the minute hand revolves another time, my grandfather walks out with my mother, his arm around her back, supporting her. Tears run down her face.

And I know my cat is gone forever.

The Tempest

Jonas's death is like a storm. Thunder booms, rain falls, lightning flashes. And then it's over. The puddles dry up, and everyone goes on their way as if it never happened.

Except me.

Our house feels different. Cold. Like it's missing its heart. I keep finding little things that remind me of him. A cat toy under my bed. A spare can of wet food in the pantry behind some black beans. His fuzzy blanket on the couch. The worst is when the orange tabby cat comes skulking around. He meows outside the cat door, waiting for Jonas to appear.

But, of course, he never does.

School is actually better than home. It's just classes, tests, and stinky gym uniforms. It's predictable, and I don't have to think or feel.

Until I see Raj waiting for me at my locker.

And I don't know why, but it actually hurts to look at him.

"Ellie," he says, his voice low, "I heard about Jonas."

"You did?" I'm surprised.

"Melvin told me." Something flickers in his eyes. "I'm really sorry."

He's *sorry*? I'm irrationally angry. At the world. At him.

"Sure you are," I mutter.

His mouth drops open. "What? I liked Jonas!"

"You liked him so much you came to see him when he got hurt, right?"

"I didn't even know!" Raj exclaims angrily. "It's not like you've been talking to me!"

"Well, you haven't been talking to me, either!" I snap.

We stare at each other.

The bell rings and I slam my locker shut.

And walk away.

It's opening night of *The Tempest*, and my mom suggests I come and see it. She says it will be a good distraction for me.

The kid playing Prospero remembers his lines, and the sets are beautiful, especially the scene at sea. The actors even get a standing ovation. But when it's over, I feel worse. Because I realize that my life has no good feels like *The Tempest*. Instead of everyone being happy and getting together in the end, everything has fallen apart—Jonas is dead, and Raj and I are broken. If Shakespeare wrote a play about me, it would be a tragedy.

We celebrate the production with takeout from my favorite Mexican place. But I'm not that hungry, even though I love burritos. It doesn't really matter, because my grandfather is eating enough for everyone.

My mom chatters away. She talks about how maybe next season she'll stage a musical. She talks about my dad and how he's going to be home this weekend. She talks and talks and talks, and the whole time I just stare at my plate. Because if I look up I'll see the empty chair across the table where Jonas used to sit, and then I'll remember the room at the vet's office and smell the sharp scent of ammonia and I'll probably be sick.

"So, I had this great idea, Ellie," my mom says. "Why don't we go to the animal shelter on Saturday and look at dogs?"

"Dogs?" I echo.

"Ben and I talked, and we decided it's fine if you want to get a dog."

"I don't want a dog."

She looks confused. "But you've always wanted a dog!"

I can't believe she's doing this.

"You can't just replace Jonas with a dog!" I shout. "He's not replaceable!"

"Of course he's not," she soothes. "You're overreacting."

I find my grandfather's words coming out of my mouth.

"I'm human! I feel deeply! And you act like everything's fine. Like Jonas was never here. Why doesn't anybody care that my cat is dead?"

"Honey, I just want to help—" my mom starts.

"I don't want to be helped! I want Jonas back!" I shout, and run out of the room.

It's the weekend, and I get to sleep in and ignore the world. The doorbell wakes me up. I feel a lump on the bed near my legs, and for a moment I think it's Jonas. Then I open my eyes and see that it's really a throw pillow.

My bedroom door opens, and then I hear a familiar voice.

"Hey, sleepyhead," my father says. "It's noon and you're still in bed?"

I'm so happy to see him. I scramble out of bed and give him a hug.

"Dad!" I say.

He ruffles my hair. "How ya doing, kiddo?"

"Not great," I say.

"Yeah, your mom said. That's hard about Jonas. He was a good cat."

"The best."

He passes me a bag.

"Got this for you on the road," he says.

I open it up. It's a night-light. It looks like a red-capped mushroom.

"Ha-ha," I say.

"I couldn't resist," he says, and grins. "So, are you going to sleep the whole day away, or do you want to get dressed and get out of here and have an adventure?"

Getting out sounds perfect.

"Adventure," I say.

○ ○ ○

We drive down the coast to Santa Cruz and go to the amusement park on the boardwalk. It's something we used to do when I was little. I thought I'd outgrown it, like animal crackers, but I'm wrong. Because it's pure fun.

There are tourists everywhere, and the air smells like popcorn and cotton candy. We gawk at the harbor seals and ride the old wooden roller coaster. My dad wins me a goldfish from one of those games of chance where you throw a Ping-Pong ball into a bowl. By the end of the day, I almost feel like myself again.

On the way home, we stop for dinner. Of course, I bring my new goldfish inside with me.

After we order, my dad and I debate what to name my new fish.

"What about Goldie?" I ask. It's what I've always named my goldfish in the past.

"Maybe try something new," he suggests.

"What about Prospero?"

"From *The Tempest*? Nice," he says, and grins. "I'm glad to see that all those nights of us reading Shakespeare to get you to fall asleep are finally paying off."

The waitress appears with our plates.

"Here we go," she says. "A BLT for the young lady and a Reuben for the gentleman."

"Thanks," my dad says.

"Oh, we ran out of regular chips, so I substituted barbecue chips," she says. "I hope you don't mind."

"Sounds delicious." My dad starts eating.

But I just stare at the chips and think of Raj. All the happiness of the day is gone in an instant, and a wave of sadness crushes me.

"Aren't you going to dig in?" my dad asks.

Tears start running down my cheeks. I can't hold it back any longer. It's a flood, a storm, a hurricane.

"Ellie, honey," my dad says worriedly. "What's wrong?"

I put my head down and cry.

For Jonas.

For Raj and me.

For everything.

Hypothesis of Us

I'm in the bathroom before school, trying to fix my hair. But no matter what I do, it doesn't look good. But then, nothing is good lately.

My grandfather calls through the door.

"Do you have a razor I can borrow?"

"Hang on," I tell him.

After searching through the cabinets, the only kind I find are the pink ones my mom uses.

"Here you go," I say, opening the door and holding one out. "It's for your legs, but it should work. . . ." My voice trails off.

Because overnight, my grandfather has grown a full beard.

He looks like Bigfoot.

"What—what—hap—?" I can't even get a sentence out.

"Apparently, our axolotl really sped up the Puberty," he says in annoyance.

"It sure did," I say.

My grandfather snatches the razor from my hand and walks down the hall.

I stand there, staring after him.

He pauses and turns around. "Do you have any shaving cream?"

"Doors open for the science fair at ten a.m. on Saturday," Mr. Ham announces to the class. "Please make sure your project is set up in the multipurpose room and ready to go by nine-forty-five. We're expecting a nice crowd."

My grandfather and I still have to write everything up, so we stay after school to work. But we're in for a rude surprise when we check on our flies: the winged ones are dying. There's a pile of dead flies on the bottom, and only a few are still clinging to the glass or flying around.

"It's a good thing the science fair is soon," my grandfather observes, looking in the jars. "I don't think the rest of them will last another week."

"Why are they dying?"

"Mold on the media," he says, pointing to the jar where there's a fuzzy patch. "It kills flies."

After everything that's happened, I can't believe the flies are dying, too! I wonder what Alexander Fleming would have to say about *this*.

"What's the point?" I snap.

"The point?"

"In even trying!" I wave at the flies. "All the experiments failed! Jonas died! And the yellow fever guys! And Grandma! And now even the fruit flies! Science didn't work for them!"

My grandfather sits back and sighs. "That's true. Those experiments did fail. But failure is part of experimentation. It's okay to make mistakes."

"It's not okay! Look what happened with Raj and me!"

He narrows his eyes. "What exactly 'happened' with Raj and you?"

All the energy seems to go out of me in a rush. I slump down on a chair and stare at the floor.

"My hypothesis was all wrong," I mutter.

"And what was your hypothesis?" my grand-father asks calmly.

"That we were perfect for each other. You know, like soul mates."

"I see." My grandfather looks thoughtful. "You're a scientist. Explain your data to me."

"We had a weird movie date. After that, we couldn't talk to each other or anything."

"So, what's your conclusion?"

"I don't know!"

"Well, were you good at being friends?"

I'm frustrated that he's even asking this. Isn't

it perfectly obvious? "We were great at being friends!"

"That sounds like a solid conclusion to me."

I look at him as I realize what he just said.

"We weren't meant to be soul mates," I say slowly. "We were meant to be *best friends* all along!"

My grandfather smiles. "Do you see? Your experiment failed, but you learned something from it."

"You're so smart!" I tell him.

"Well, I do have two PhDs," he says.

I hug him tight.

"Now let's get to work on this science project," he says. "By the way, you are far too young to be dating. Teenage boys have very sweaty hands, you know."

Movies and plays always have big scenes where a character declares their undying love to someone else. Nobody writes stories where they declare their undying friendship. Maybe Romeo and Juliet would've had a happy ending if they'd just been friends in the first place.

I don't know how to go about approaching Raj. Do I call him? Text him? Do I ask him to meet me for coffee? In the end, I put a bag of barbecue chips in his locker as a peace offering. I don't even leave a note, because he'll know what it means.

But as the morning drags on, I start to worry. What if we're too far gone? What if our friendship has been destroyed in this experiment? My stomach gets tighter and tighter. And then I step out on the lunch court and see him sitting at our regular table.

With an empty seat across from him.

I walk over and slide into the chair wordlessly.

"Hey," he says.

"Hey," I say back.

We both sit there for a minute.

"I think we should go back to the way it was before," I blurt out. "Being friends."

A look of relief crosses his face.

"Good idea," he agrees.

We both grin.

"Want a chip?" he asks. "I found them in my locker."

"Someone just put potato chips in your locker? I wonder who did it?"

"It's a mystery," he says with a smile. Then he says, "So, I'm thinking of getting all of my hair dyed."

"Really?"

He nods.

"What color?"

"I'm not sure. Maybe magenta."

"Just make sure it's not green. You don't want to look like a leprechaun."

He laughs.

We sit there and debate hair color and eat barbecue chips until the bell rings.

Because that's what best friends do.

Prizes

Saturday morning arrives, and I don't get to sleep in late because it's the science fair. My mom surprises my grandfather and me with matching white lab coats.

"Where'd you get these?" I ask her.

"Aren't they adorable?" she raves. "I had one of my wardrobe friends find them."

There's embroidery on the pocket. It says:

TEAM MELLIE

"Mellie?" my grandfather asks.

"Melvin plus Ellie equals Mellie. Cute, right?"

My grandfather and I share a look.

"Maybe we're a new species?" I say.

The science fair is set up in the multipurpose room, and there's a huge turnout of kids from all over the county. The projects are pretty cool, and range from measuring raindrops to recycling trash, to baking-soda-and-vinegar rockets. Quite a few kids have grown mold. I guess mold is more popular than I realized.

Still, I can't help but feel a little sad to be standing in this crowded room. Because even though my project with Grandpa succeeded more than we ever imagined, we can't display it. My grandfather says—and I agree—that our discovery is too much for a middle school science fair.

Instead, we've deliberately presented only one aspect of our experiment.

Mr. Ham walks over and checks out our table.

"'The Effect of Hot-Lunch Chicken Nuggets on the Growth of Fruit Flies,'" he reads. "Interesting."

"Thanks," I say.

"What were your findings?" he asks.

"The fruit flies that ate the chicken nugget media died faster than the ones who didn't," I say.

"I'm not surprised," he says, and winks. "Why do you think teachers always bring their lunch to school?"

In the end, we don't get a prize. We don't even get an honorable mention. Some kid who made a battery using a potato wins. I try to comfort myself that at least I'm getting extra credit, but I still feel a little disappointed.

"It's not fair," I say. "We grew an appendix."

My grandfather and I are in the kitchen eating microwave burritos. He tries to cheer me up.

"Real scientists are never recognized in their time. Did you know that nobody paid much attention to Alexander Fleming when he first discovered penicillin?"

"Really?"

"It's true," he says. "And he wasn't honored with a Nobel until seventeen years later."

"I have to wait seventeen years? I'll be an old lady by then."

He just looks at me. "Excuse me," he says. "You did not just say that."

The doorbell rings and I answer it.

It's our neighbor, and he's holding the big orange tabby cat.

"Hi," he says. "Is your mom home?"

My mom comes to the door a moment later.

"Sorry I haven't been over before," the neighbor apologizes. "I work in tech and keep kind of crazy hours. I'm Art."

"Nice to meet you," my mom says. "I'm Lissa and this is Ellie."

"So, this is kind of hello and good-bye," Art says, looking awkward. "I just got a gig in Singapore. I'm leaving the day after tomorrow."

"Congratulations!" my mom says. "That sounds exciting."

"Thanks! It is," Art says. "Anyway, I wanted to stop by before I left. Connor here is always playing with your cat."

"Our cat died," I say. "Jonas got hit by a car."

"Oh, wow, sorry to hear that," Art says. "I was wondering why I hadn't seen him around lately."

We don't say anything.

Then Art says, "I can't take Connor with me. I thought I'd see if you wanted him before I took him to the animal shelter."

"The shelter?" my mom asks.

Art looks apologetic. "None of my friends can take him. I've tried everyone I know. You guys were my last hope."

I look at the cat. He's not a kitten. He's older. He's the cat equivalent of what you find in the Lost and Found box: something left behind and forgotten.

My mom hesitates. "I'm not sure we're ready for another cat just yet. If you know what I mean."

"Sure, of course," Art says quickly. "Anyway, it was worth a shot. Nice to have met you. Sorry about your cat and all."

"Can I maybe hold him for a minute?" I ask.

"Sure," Art says.

He places the fat orange tabby cat in my arms.

"Try him out," he says. "See if you like him."

It's funny how he says it. As if you can "try out" a cat like it's a bike or a car.

"It's up to you, Ellie," my mom says.

It feels nice to hold a cat again, but a familiar feeling pricks at my stomach. What if I'm making a mistake? What if something happens to this cat? What if he gets hit by a car? What if he dies? What if—

Then the cat starts purring.

Like magic, my doubts melt away and a warm lump settles close to my heart.

"We'll keep him," I say.

Maybe I got a prize after all.

It feels like Herschel's always been part of our family. He didn't seem like much of a Connor, so I gave him a new name. I think it suits him. Because he's always looking out at the sky. The windowsill is his favorite place to sit.

Herschel has his own quirks. He usually hides when the doorbell rings. He's never met a moth he doesn't want to bat down. He alternates who he sleeps with at night between me and my mother and my grandfather, like he's spreading out his love. But mostly, Herschel really likes to eat. And he's happy to let you know.

When I walk in the front door a week or so later, he starts meowing right away. It's late, almost dinnertime. Raj and I hung out at a local park and ended up watching the old men playing chess. Raj did a play-by-play of the action like a sportscaster. The old men loved it and gave him a few pro tips.

"Okay, okay," I tell my cat. "I'll feed you."

He trails me into the kitchen. The rest of the house is quiet. My mom is still at school, and my grandfather is probably sleeping. He had a head-ache this morning and stayed home from school.

Herschel is insistent, nudging me toward the

pantry drawer. His meowing gets louder and louder. I open a can of wet food and am spooning it into a bowl when I hear heavy footsteps. I look up to see a bald man walking into the kitchen.

I'm so startled that I scream and throw the can of cat food at him.

"Ellie," he says, waving his hands. "It's me!"

That's when I realize that the man standing in the kitchen doorway is my *grandfather*!

And he looks like a grandfather now.

Interesting Result

"What happened?" I ask him.

He sighs. "I guess you could say this is an interesting result."

"You took more of the axolotl?" I ask him.

He looks a little ashamed. "After my appendix, I couldn't resist! I really wanted a new tooth. Dentures are terrible!"

"But why did it make you grow old? I don't understand. . . ."

"The fruit flies didn't die from mold," he says. "Our axolotl made *everything* grow faster."

I think of his beard.

"The fruit flies died of old age," I say slowly.

"Correct."

Panic rushes through me. "Wait a minute! Does this mean you're going to die of old age, too?"

"Of course I will," he says, and then his face softens. "Someday. But I don't think anytime soon."

"How can you know?"

"Because fruit flies don't live very long to begin with. Losing a week for them is like losing twenty years for us. Using that calculation, I'll likely live to my eighties at least."

"How old do you think you are now?"

"No arthritis. My knees don't ache. I feel like I did when I was in my late fifties."

"But you're bald!"

He rolls his eyes. "Ellie, I started going bald in my thirties. Baldness has nothing to do with age and everything to do with genetics."

Science is weird. It can make you young. It can make you old. It can make you bald.

The garage door rumbles open, and I hear my

mom's car pull in. A minute later, she walks in carrying a pizza.

"We finished striking the set in record time, so I stopped and grabbed a pizza—" She freezes when she sees my grandfather.

The pizza falls to the floor with a splat and slides out of the cardboard container.

"Dad! You're old again!"

"Thank you for pointing out the obvious." He looks at the floor. "What kind of pizza did you get?"

"Uh, veggie lovers'," she says.

"No great loss," he says. Then he grabs the car keys out of her hand and walks out. "I need to borrow your car."

"Wait!" she calls. "Where are you going?"

"To get another pizza," my grandfather says. "A real one. With pepperoni."

The door slams and he's gone.

My mom looks at the pizza and then at me and shakes her head.

○ ○ ○

The first thing my grandfather does is buy a new car.

Or, rather, an *old* car.

"What do you think? It's a 1955 Ford Thunderbird in Aquatone Blue," my grandfather tells us in a proud voice.

It's a light-blue convertible with big round red taillights and white-rimmed wheels.

We stand in the driveway and admire it.

"Just like the one you always wanted, huh?" I ask.

"Does this thing even have airbags?" my mom asks.

"It's got a V-8 engine!" my grandfather says. "Hop in. We're taking a Sunday drive."

When we get onto the highway, my grandfather guns the engine.

"Let's see how fast this baby can go," he says, a gleam in his eye.

"Dad," my mom says. "Take it easy."

But he speeds up and we're flying down the highway. People wave at us as we whiz by. The car is eye-catching.

Maybe a little *too* eye-catching.

Because a moment later, I hear a siren. I look back and see a police cruiser with flashing lights. Once we're on the side of the road, the police officer walks to the driver's side.

"License and registration, please," the officer says.

My grandfather hands them over without a word. The police officer looks from the driver's license back to my grandfather.

"You look great for being seventy-seven, Mr. Sagarsky," the police officer says.

"Good genes," my grandfather says.

"Sir, you were doing seventy in a fifty-five zone," the officer says. "In the carpool lane."

"Sorry. I guess I was a little excited. I just got the car," my grandfather explains.

The officer studies the car. "V-8 engine, huh?"

"Purrs like a kitten. Want to try it out?"

My mom smacks her head.

Now, instead of me having to take the bus home from school, my grandfather picks me up in Big Betty. That's what he's named his car. Usually we go and get a snack afterward at the little sandwich shop. One thing that *hasn't* changed is his appetite.

I sit across from him as he powers his way through a triple-decker turkey club, a meatball sandwich, a bowl of clam chowder, a slice of coconut cream pie, and black coffee.

"This pie is delicious," he says, pushing the plate to me. "You should try it!"

Now that he's back to his *old* self, he seems lighter. Happier.

"Do you like being old?" I ask him.

"It's fine," he says with a shrug. "To be honest, I wasn't looking forward to having to take the SATs again in high school."

"Hello, Ellie," a voice says.

I turn around to see Mrs. Barrymore standing there. It's always weird seeing teachers outside of school, even though my mom is one.

Mrs. Barrymore's eyes flit to my grandfather.

"This is my grandfather, Dr. Sagarsky," I say. "Grandpa, this is Mrs. Barrymore. She's the librarian at my school."

My grandfather stands and shakes her hand. "Very pleased to meet you. My grandson, Melvin, speaks very highly of you."

"Well, I think the world of him. How is he doing?"

My mother told the middle school that her "nephew" had moved back to Fresno.

"Uh, he's doing fine," my grandfather says. "Thank you for asking."

"We miss having him around."

My grandfather . . . blushes?

"How long are you visiting for?"

"Oh. I recently moved to the area." He nods at me. "To be closer to Ellie and her mom."

"How nice," Mrs. Barrymore says. "I guess we'll be seeing more of you, then?"

"Yes," he says.

She looks at his plate. "How is the coconut cream pie?"

"I highly recommend it," he says.

"I'll have to try it," she tells him. "I need to be going. I have an appointment. It was nice running into you, Ellie."

I nod.

To my grandfather she says, "Be sure to give Melvin my best if you talk to him."

"I will," he promises.

After she leaves, my grandfather turns to me. His face is a little green.

"Are you okay?"

"I think I need an antacid," he says, and looks down at the empty dishes. "Seems like my stomach got old, too."

Comet

The middle school parking lot is like a fishbowl where the fish are rushing around trying to get out. I'm sitting with Raj after school, waiting for my grandfather to pick me up.

"Do you want to do something Saturday night?" I ask him.

"Movie?"

I have something different in mind.

"Comet."

He raises an eyebrow. "Comet?"

I explain how I've become completely obsessed

with Caroline Herschel, and that I really want to see a comet.

"Sure, that sounds kinda cool," he says.

"Great," I tell him.

My grandfather walks up to us, shaking his head.

"This place smells like the Puberty," he says.

His eyes widen when he sees Raj's head. "You dyed your hair *blue*?"

"Do you like it?" Raj asks him.

"At least it's not permanent," my grandfather says.

Then he walks past us into the school.

"Wait! Where are you going?" I call after him. "I thought you were taking me home?"

He holds up a book. *To Kill a Mockingbird.* "I need to return this to the library. I'll be right back."

"I gotta run, too," Raj says. "Chess."

Then I'm all alone. While I wait, I play a test version of Ben's new game on my phone. He sent it to me last night. It's pretty cute, and I can't help but notice that the girl character looks like my mom.

I'm so engrossed that when I look up, I realize I've been sitting there for a half hour. How long does it take to return a library book?

I decide to go get my grandfather.

When I walk in, I see him sitting at a table with Mrs. Barrymore, the book between them. She says something and he smiles.

It's kind of odd. My grandfather's normal resting face is grumpy. But this is different.

This smile transforms his face.

"How was the comet-watching?" my mom asks me as we fold clothes.

"We didn't see any," I tell her.

It was a little disappointing. It turns out that comets are not like stars. They're rare. They only show up once in a while, and you have to be in the right place at the right time to see them. Even then, they may be hard to spot.

My mom holds up one of my grandfather's shirts.

"Well, it's not like he has to buy a new wardrobe," she says with a laugh. "He was already rocking the whole old-man thing."

"You think he's ever going to do his own laundry instead of sneaking it in with ours?"

"I imagine he will," she says. "He's getting his own place. He told me last night."

"What? He is? Why?"

She looks at me. "Ben's coming home for good in three weeks. Your grandfather thinks it's time for him to get his own bedroom."

I'm not sure how I feel about this.

"Where's he going to live?"

"He says he wants to stay around here."

"I'll miss having him in the house," I say.

"I won't," she says. "I want the den back."

I look at her. "But I'll miss him."

"You can see him all you want, sweetie," she says gently. "He's a grown man. It's time for him to figure things out."

But I wonder. Does anyone ever really figure things out?

My grandfather's apartment is just a one-bedroom, but he's excited about it.

"Maybe I'll get a pet," he muses.

"A cat?" I ask.

"Maybe a rat. Rats are interesting pets. They're very smart, you know."

"I feel like I'm sending you off to college or something," my mom confesses as we help him pack up his stuff.

On moving day, we load up the boxes in my mom's van and drive to his new apartment. The place has nice wood floors and is bright, with freshly painted walls. He's already bought some basic furniture—a couch, a coffee table, a kitchen table, and a bedroom set.

"This is really nice, Dad," my mom says, looking around.

We spend the afternoon helping my grandfather put his bookcases together and unpacking. My mom can't believe he didn't bother to buy any cleaning supplies, so she heads out to do some shopping for him.

I put my grandmother's romance novels on a shelf. My grandfather puts a wedding photo of them next to it. It's sweet.

"What are you going to do now?" I ask him.

He knows I'm talking about his life.

"I'm not sure I want to go back into research. I'm thinking about teaching," he admits.

"Middle school?"

"You couldn't pay me a million dollars to teach middle school," he says.

Me either.

"High school might be more appropriate," he says.

"I think you'd be a great teacher," I tell him.

"You've always been my best student," he says with a fond look.

I pick up *The Burning Sands*.

"Can I borrow this one?" I ask him.

"Of course," he says. "Just don't get any ideas about running away with a sheikh."

My grandfather always seems to have an excuse to swing by the library to visit Mrs. Barrymore when he picks me up after school. He'll bring her a book he thinks she might like. Or a bag of old-fashioned candy—peppermint sticks.

Today, he's brought her a feather he found when he was out walking. They pore over bird books, their heads bent together, trying to identify the feather.

That's when it hits me: my grandfather is flirting with her.

He whistles on the drive home. When he pulls into our driveway, I turn to him.

"Do you like Mrs. Barrymore?" I ask him.

"Uh, ahem, Eleanor's very nice."

"You should ask her out on a date."

My grandfather's face turns white. "A date? I can't do *that*."

"Why not?"

"Because, because . . ." His voice trails off.

"You told me it's important to experiment."

"But this is *different*," he insists.

"It might not be as bad as you think. Like me and the mushrooms."

"What are you talking about?"

"I didn't like mushrooms the first two times I tried them. But the third time, I had this vegetarian lasagna with portobello mushrooms, and it was delicious."

"Are you seriously comparing my, my—*life!*—to mushrooms?"

I look at him.

"I think she likes you, too," I say softly.

He grips the steering wheel tightly. "What if it doesn't work out?"

"But what if it does? What if Mrs. Barrymore is like a comet?"

"A comet?" he asks with a confused look.

"Rare." I pause. "They don't come around all the time."

We sit there in the car in silence.

Then he sighs.

"You know, you're a very wise young lady," he says.

"I must take after my grandfather," I tell him, and grin. "He has two PhDs."

Experiment

Mrs. Barrymore says she'd love to go to lunch with my grandfather.

But the day before the big date, my grandfather shows up at our house in a panic.

Raj and I are doing homework at the kitchen table and eating my latest quiche—mushroom and spinach. I'm kind of over tofu. And in spite of everything that's happened, we're still perfect quiche eaters.

We watch my grandfather as he paces back and forth.

"It's so nerve-racking!" he exclaims. "What do we talk about? The last time I went on a date, I had hair!"

"What do you usually talk about?" Raj asks.

"Well, lately we've been discussing finches."

"What's a finch?" I ask.

"It's a bird."

"That's easy, then," Raj says. "Talk about birds."

"We can't talk about birds for two hours!" My grandfather stares at the floor. "This is going to be a complete disaster."

I guess even grown-ups get nervous about dating.

"I have an idea," I tell him. "What if Raj and I come, too?"

He looks confused. "On the date?"

"More people. Less pressure," I explain. "It's easier in a group."

His face brightens. "Yes! That's an excellent idea. Thank you."

I smile.

"Now I just have one problem left."

"What?"

He frowns. "I have absolutely no idea what to wear."

In the end, he wears a navy-blue suit with a burgundy bow tie.

"Looking swag, Melvin," Raj compliments him.

"It's not too much?" he asks nervously.

"I like the pocket square," I tell him.

We go to the 1950s restaurant. When Mrs. Barrymore walks in, it's clear that she's made an effort, too. She's wearing another retro dress and fits right in with the decor.

My grandfather holds out Mrs. Barrymore's seat for her before she sits down. It's sweet and old-fashioned.

"I've been wanting to try out this place," Mrs. Barrymore says, looking around. "I hear they make very good hamburgers."

"Just don't order it medium rare," Raj jokes.

My grandfather clears his throat. "So, I'm considering teaching."

"Really?" Mrs. Barrymore says with a smile. "That's wonderful! We desperately need more people teaching who are excited about science."

"And he's got two PhDs," I say.

"I'm so impressed! I had no idea."

My grandfather's face just keeps getting redder and redder. I think even his bald head is starting to turn red.

We look at the menus.

"I think I want a malted," I say. "Chocolate."

"They have malteds?" Mrs. Barrymore asks.

"Yes," my grandfather says.

Mrs. Barrymore makes a happy sound. "I haven't had a malted since I was a young girl. The drive-in we used to go to made the best ones."

"I miss drive-ins," my grandfather muses.

"What's a drive-in?" Raj asks.

Mrs. Barrymore and my grandfather burst out laughing like they're sharing a private joke, and maybe they are. Like Brianna and me. These two old people have both missed having someone else to *remember* with.

When my grandfather catches his breath, he explains.

"A drive-in is an outdoor movie theater. You used to drive to it in your car and park there to watch it."

"You'd watch a movie in your car?" I ask. "That doesn't sound very comfortable."

"Oh, it was just wonderful!" Mrs. Barrymore exclaims. "There's nothing quite like watching a movie under the open sky."

Raj gives me a look. "The old days were weird."

Mrs. Barrymore and my grandfather ignore us.

"You know what I don't understand about this generation?" my grandfather asks her. "There's no good music."

"I couldn't agree more," she says. "Do they even use real instruments anymore? My students tell me they make music on the computer these days."

They talk like they've known each other forever.

That's when I know that magic truly exists. But

it has nothing to do with fairies or spells or wizards. Magic is accident and chance. It's something unexpected. Like mold in a petri dish or a fat, purring orange cat.

Or maybe even love.

I've been working my way through my grandmother's romance books. They're kind of addicting. I see why she liked them so much.

But I wish someone would invent a new category of books: on friendship. The books could have their own section in the bookstore, like fantasy or history. They could call it Friendmance or maybe Friend Fiction.

Because friendship is as important as romance. You can have a bad day with a friend. You can eat barbecue chips with them. You can count on them to help you survive middle school.

Just like in the natural world, friends come in all different genus and species. There are best friends, like Raj. And there are old friends, like Brianna, who are important, too. It's nice to have someone remind you about the good feels of kindergarten and animal crackers.

Then, of course, there are friends who defy classification. Like my grandfather. I'd even say he's a new species all his own: favorite person (*Favorite personus*?).

Because he taught me that failure is okay. That experimentation is important in science.

And in life.

Which is why I'm sitting in a chair in the hair salon getting a streak dyed in my hair. I still think blue is a mistake, though.

I went for pink instead.

Author's Note

I have always been fascinated by the story of penicillin. Maybe because I'm a doctor's kid.

But I also loved the idea of a scientist accidentally discovering a medicine that changed the course of the modern world. As Melvin would say: talk about an interesting result! Not to mention that Sir Alexander Fleming and I have a lot in common. (You should see my messy desk.)

As I dug further into Fleming and his "accidental mould," I learned that the discovery was just the beginning of the story. Because although Alexander Fleming discovered *Penicillium notatum* in 1928, it would take fourteen years and hard work by many other scientists to develop it into a practical antibiotic. Penicillin was successfully used to treat a patient in 1942. In 1945, Alexander Fleming shared the Nobel Prize in Physiology or Medicine with Howard Florey and Ernst Chain. A preserved

specimen of Fleming's "mould" can still be viewed at the Science Museum in London, England.

Maybe the real lesson of penicillin is that success—like life—is a mix of hard work, failure, and even a little magic.

So be adventurous like a scientist. Try new things. Don't be afraid to make mistakes. It's part of the process of discovery.

And always look for the unexpected in the world around you.

Acknowledgments

With warm thanks to my editor, Michelle Nagler, for continuing to let me experiment. Also, to Shannon Rosa for teaching me how to hunt mushrooms.

Recommended Resources for Continuing the Conversation

Alexander Fleming and Penicillin
nobelprize.org/nobel_prizes/medicine/laureates /1945/fleming-bio.html
Caroline and William Herschel
McCully, Emily Arnold. *Caroline's Comets.* New York: Holiday House, 2017.
Antonie van Leeuwenhoek
www.history-of-the-microscope.org/anton-van -leeuwenhoek-microscope-history.php

Carolus Linnaeus

linnean.org/education-resources/who-was-linnaeus

Mistakes

Jones, Charlotte Foltz. *Mistakes That Worked: The World's Familiar Inventions and How They Came to Be.* New York: Delacorte Press, 2016.

Scientists

Fortey, Jacqueline. *DK Eyewitness: Great Scientists.* London: DK Publishing, 2007.

Yellow Fever

Anderson, Laurie Halse. *Fever 1793.* New York: Simon & Schuster Books for Young Readers, 2002.

Mellie's Gallery of Scientists

James Carroll and Jesse Lazear

CARROLL LIVED: 1854–1907

LAZEAR LIVED: 1866–1900

CARROLL'S BIRTHPLACE: Woolwich, England

LAZEAR'S BIRTHPLACE: Baltimore, Maryland

SCIENTIFIC INTERESTS: Bacteriology, virology

NOTABLE ACHIEVEMENTS: Yellow fever was a deadly disease. Carroll and Lazear were two doctors on the US Army Yellow Fever Commission, which was studying the disease. A hypothesis known as the mosquito theory suggested that yellow fever was spread by the insects. Both Carroll and Lazear deliberately allowed an infected mosquito to bite them, and they contracted the disease. Carroll recovered from yellow fever, but it badly damaged his heart. Lazear died of yellow fever.

INVENTION: Proved that mosquitoes transmitted yellow fever

CARROLL QUOTE: "Four days later, I had fever, and on the day following I was carried to the isolation camp as a patient with yellow fever."

LAZEAR QUOTE: "I rather think I am on the track of the real germ."

Alexander Fleming

LIVED: 1881–1955

BIRTHPLACE: Ayrshire, Scotland

CHILDHOOD: Fleming's parents were farmers, and he appreciated the natural world.

SCIENTIFIC INTERESTS: Bacteriology, immunology

NOTABLE ACHIEVEMENTS: Fleming discovered the first true antibiotic—penicillin. He noticed that a mold had stopped the growth of a bacteria in a culture plate. He originally called it "mould juice." He would share the Nobel Prize for Physiology or Medicine for the discovery and development of penicillin.

INVENTION: Discovery of penicillin

QUOTE: "I certainly didn't plan to revolutionize all medicine by discovering the world's first antibiotic, or bacteria killer. But I suppose that was exactly what I did."

Caroline Herschel

LIVED: 1750–1848

BIRTHPLACE: Hanover, Germany

CHILDHOOD: Caroline was a singer, and her brother William was a musician. They often performed together.

SCIENTIFIC INTEREST: Astronomy

NOTABLE ACHIEVEMENTS: Caroline, who left Germany for England in 1772, began her career by assisting her astronomer brother, William. She went on to become the first woman to discover a comet. Caroline was also the first female professional astronomer, as she was paid a salary. She was awarded a gold medal by the Royal Astronomical Society.

INVENTION: Discovered comets and cataloged stars and nebulae

QUOTE: "This evening I saw an object which I believe will prove to-morrow night to be a comet."

William Herschel

LIVED: 1738–1822

BIRTHPLACE: Hanover, Germany

CHILDHOOD: William was the son of
a musician, and he could play the oboe,
harpsichord, violin, and organ.

SCIENTIFIC INTEREST: Astronomy

NOTABLE ACHIEVEMENTS: After
moving to England, William constructed
his own telescopes to look at the sky. He
discovered the planet Uranus. Because
of this discovery, he was knighted by
King George III and was appointed court
astronomer. Aided by his sister Caroline,
he cataloged over 2,500 nebulae and star
clusters.

INVENTION: Discovery of Uranus

QUOTE: "I have looked further into space
than ever human being did before me. I have
observed stars of which the light, it can be
proved, must take two million years to reach
the earth."

Antonie van Leeuwenhoek

LIVED: 1632–1723

BIRTHPLACE: Delft, Dutch Republic (the Netherlands)

CHILDHOOD: Van Leeuwenhoek had a hard childhood. When he was quite young, his father died, and he was sent away to school.

SCIENTIFIC INTERESTS: Microbiology, microscopy

NOTABLE ACHIEVEMENTS: Known as the Father of Microbiology, Van Leeuwenhoek was the first person to observe the microscopic world. He constructed powerful microscopes and observed microorganisms such as bacteria, which he called "animalcules."

INVENTION: Discovery and observation of the microscopic world

QUOTE: "Whenever I found out anything remarkable, I have thought it my duty to put down my discovery on paper, so that all ingenious people might be informed thereof."

Carolus Linnaeus

LIVED: 1707–1788

BIRTHPLACE: Råshult, Sweden

CHILDHOOD: Linnaeus did not enjoy studying and preferred to look at plants.

SCIENTIFIC INTERESTS: Botany, zoology

NOTABLE ACHIEVEMENTS: Linnaeus
created a formal system of identifying and
classifying the natural world and established
a uniform naming structure.

INVENTION: Created the taxonomy
system of binomial nomenclature (two
names).

QUOTE: "If you do not know the names of
things, the knowledge of them is lost too."

AN EXPERIMENT IN POSSIBILITY

"Warm, witty and wise." —*The New York Times*

Three-Time Newbery Honor–Winning Author

JENNIFER L. HOLM

A *New York Times* Bestseller

THE FOURTEENTH GOLDFISH

BELIEVE IN THE ~~IMPOSSIBLE~~ POSSIBLE

Read on in case you missed
The Fourteenth Goldfish!

Ring

Warm air drifts through my bedroom window. We live in the Bay Area, in the shadow of San Francisco, and late-September nights can be cool. But it's hot tonight, like summer is refusing to leave.

I used to love how my bedroom was decorated, but lately I'm not so sure. The walls are covered with the painted handprints of me and my best friend, Brianna. We started doing them back in first grade and added more handprints every year. You can see my little handprints grow bigger, like a time capsule of my life.

But we haven't done any yet this school year, or even this summer, because Brianna found her passion: volleyball. She's busy every second now with clinics and practices and weekend tournaments. The truth is, I'm not even sure if she's still my best friend.

It's late when the garage door finally grinds open. I hear my mother talking to Nicole in the front hall, and I go to them.

"Thanks for staying," she tells Nicole.

My mom looks frazzled. Her mascara is smudged beneath her eyes, her red lipstick chewed away. Her natural hair color is dirty blond like mine, but she colors it. Right now, it's purple.

"No problem," Nicole replies. "Is your dad okay?"

An unreadable expression crosses my mom's face. "Oh, he's fine. Thanks for asking. Do you need a ride home?"

"I'm good!" Nicole says. "By the way, Lissa, I have some exciting news!"

"Yes?"

"I got a job at the mall! Isn't that great?"

"I didn't know you were looking," my mom says, confused.

"Yeah, I didn't think I'd get it. It's such a big opportunity. The ear-piercing place at the mall!"

"When do you start?" my mom asks.

"That's the hard part. They want me to start tomorrow afternoon. So I can't watch Ellie anymore. I totally would have given you more notice, but . . ."

"I understand," my mom says, and I can hear the strain in her voice.

Nicole turns to me. "I forgot to tell you. I get a discount! Isn't that great? So come by anytime and shop."

"Uh, okay," I say.

"I better be going," she says. "Good night!"

"Good night," my mother echoes.

I stand in the doorway with my mother and watch her walk out into the night.

"Did she just quit?" I ask. I'm a little in shock.

My mother nods. "This is turning into a banner day."

I stare out into the night to catch a last glimpse of my babysitter, but see someone else: a boy with long hair. He's standing beneath the old, dying palm tree on our front lawn. It drops big brown fronds everywhere, and my mom says it needs to come down.

The boy is slender, wiry-looking. He looks thirteen, maybe fourteen? It's hard to tell with boys sometimes.

"You need to put your trash out," the boy calls to my mom. Tomorrow is trash day and our neighbors' trash cans line the street.

"Would you please come inside already?" my mom tells the boy.

"And when's the last time you fertilized the lawn?" he asks. "There's crabgrass."

"It's late," my mom says, holding the door open impatiently.

I wonder if he's one of my mom's students. Sometimes they help her haul stuff in and out of her big, battered cargo van.

"You have to maintain your house if you want it to maintain its value," he says.

"Now!"

The boy reluctantly picks up a large duffel bag and walks into our house.

He doesn't look like the typical theater-crew kid. They usually wear jeans and T-shirts, stuff that's easy to work in. This kid's wearing a rumpled pinstripe shirt, khaki polyester pants, a tweed jacket with patches on the elbows, and leather loafers. But it's his socks that stand out the most: they're black dress socks. You don't see boys in middle school wearing those a lot. It's like he's on his way to a bar mitzvah.

He stares at me with piercing eyes.

"Did you make honor roll?"

I'm startled, but answer anyway.

"Uh, we haven't gotten report cards yet."

Something about the boy seems familiar. His hair is dark brown, on the shaggy side, and the ends are dyed gray. An actor from one of my mom's shows, maybe?

"Who are you?" I ask him.

He ignores me.

"You need good grades if you're going to get into a competitive PhD program."

"PhD program? She's eleven years old!" my mother says.

"You can't start too early. Speaking of which," he says, looking pointedly at my mother's outfit, "is *that* what you wear to work?"

My mom likes to raid the theater wardrobe closet at school. This morning, she left the house in a floor-length black satin skirt and matching bolero jacket with a frilly white poet's shirt.

"Maybe you should consider buying a nice pant-suit," he suggests.

"Still stuck in the Stone Age, I see," she shoots back.

Then he turns and looks at me, taking in my tank-top-and-boxer-shorts pajama set.

He says, "Why are your pajamas so short? Whatever happened to long nightgowns? Are you boy-crazy like your mother was?"

"All the girls her age wear pajamas like that," my mom answers for me. "And I wasn't boy-crazy!"

"You must've been boy-crazy to elope," he says.

"I was in love," she says through gritted teeth.

"A PhD lasts a lot longer than love," he replies. "It's not too late to go back to school. You could still get a real degree."

Something about this whole exchange tickles my memory. It's like watching a movie I've alr seen. I study the boy—the gray-tipped hair, the way he's standing so comfortably in our hall, how his right hand opens and closes as if used to grasping something by habit. But it's the heavy gold ring hanging loosely on his middle finger that draws my eye. It's a school ring, like the kind you get in college, and it looks old and worn and has a red gem in the center.

"I've seen that ring before," I say, and then I remember whose hand I saw it on.

I look at the boy.

"Grandpa?" I blurt out.

Grown-ups lie.
That's one truth Beans knows for sure.

Turn the page to start reading!

JULY 1934
LYING LIARS

Look here, Mac. I'm gonna give it to you straight: grown-ups lie.

Sure, they like to say that kids make things up and that we don't tell the truth. But they're the lying liars.

Take President Roosevelt. He's been saying on the radio that the economy was improving, when anyone with two eyes could see the only thing getting better was my mother's ability to patch holes in pants. Not that she had a choice. There was no money for new threads with Poppy out of work. It was either that or let us go naked.

Then there was Winky. He was the lyingest liar of them all.

"You said twenty cans for a dime, Winky!" I pointed at the small red wagon.

It was full of empty condensed-milk cans. I found them for Winky and cleaned them up. Even smoothed the sharp edges. Winky sold the cans to Pepe's Café, where they used them to serve *café con leche*—espresso and condensed milk. Everyone in Key West drank leche, even toddlers.

"You must have wax in your ears, Beans," Winky replied. He had a potbelly and slicked-back, greasy hair that matched his slippery ways. The armpits of his Cuban-style shirt were stained yellow. "I said *fifty* cans."

I was so burned up by his words that steam just about burst out of my ears. And believe me, it was sweltering outside. Key West in July was stinking hot.

Especially stinking.

Garbage had been piling up ever since the town ran out of money to pay for collecting it. Flies swarmed above the rotting mounds. They were filthy and disgusting, and my brother and I had spent the entire morning in them.

Me and Kermit had dug through steaming piles of

garbage from one side of Key West to the other, looking for milk cans. We'd dodged stray dogs and mosquitoes and fearless rats. I couldn't imagine a worse job
in the whole world. Except maybe cleaning outhouses.

Now Winky was trying to cheat us out of our money?

"I heard you just fine," I told him. "You said *twenty*."

"Sorry, but you're full of beans, Beans," Winky said,
and then laughed. "Look: I made a joke. Get it? *Full of
beans?*"

"Hilarious," I said, and glared. "You're a regular
comedian, Winky."

"I suppose I could give you a nickel for twenty,"
Winky offered us, like he was a king doing us a favor.

"A nickel?" I wasn't very good at arithmetic, but
even I knew that this was a lousy deal.

"Sorry, Beans," Winky added with a smirk. "Maybe
you can find someone else to sell the cans to?"

I glared at him. I would if I could, but everyone
knew that Winky had the only milk can game in town.
He was a cousin of Pepe's.

"Beans," Kermit whined, tugging on my shirt. "I'm
hungry."

I sighed and rolled my eyes. Kermit wore crooked
glasses and couldn't drive a bargain with a kitten.

Winky saw the advantage and took it. A fake kindly expression lit up his face. "Why, Beans. Your little brother's hungry. I bet a nickel would buy a nice lunch."

I swallowed my pride.

"Fine," I muttered. "We'll take the nickel."

"What's that?" Winky asked loudly. "I didn't quite hear you."

I glared at him.

"I said we'll take the nickel!"

He dropped the coin into my outstretched palm.

"C'mon, Kermit," I snapped. "Let's go."

As we walked away, Winky shouted, "Always a pleasure doing business with you, Beans!"

I'd been Winkied again.